SHERLOCK & DRACULA

LIFEBLOOD

By Kev Freeman

Based on characters developed by Sir Arthur Conan Doyle and by Bram Stoker

Cover Design by MiblArt

The Sherlock-Dracula Lifeblood Novel is a work of fiction.

Beyond the names, characters, businesses, places, events, locales, and incidents first created by Sir Arthur Conan Doyle within his works of Sherlock Holmes together with those created by Bram Stoker in his works of Dracula, all other names, characters, businesses, places, events, locales, and incidents are either the products of the author's imagination or used in a fictitious manner. Any resemblance to actual persons, living or dead, or actual events is purely coincidental.

ISBN: 978-1-7365709-3-7 (e-book)
ISBN: 978-1-7365709-4-4 (paperback)
ISBN: 978-1-7365709-5-1 (hardback)

PREFACE

Lifeblood is built upon the works of Dracula, written by Bram Stoker and The Adventures of Sherlock Holmes (and other stories), written by Sir Arthur Conan Doyle. The novel pits the characters created in those classic works against each other in an epic battle pushing gothic vampire horror against classic detective. The story is set in 1894 Victorian London, seven years after Dracula had been dispatched at the hands of Jonathan Harker and his comrades in the Carpathian Mountains. Through an unexpected visit, Sherlock Holmes and Dr. Watson are commissioned to locate the lair of the Count and prevent his vengeance upon those who believed they had slain him.

PROLOGUE

'Seven years ago, we all went through the flames; and the happiness of some of us since then is, we think, well worth the pain we endured. It is an added joy to Mina and to me that our boy's birthday is the same day as that on which Quincey Morris died. His mother holds, I know, the secret belief that some of our brave friend's spirit has passed into him. His bundle of names links all our little band of men together; but we call him Quincey.

In the summer of this year, we made a journey to Transylvania, and went over the old ground which was, and is, to us so full of vivid and terrible memories. It was almost impossible to believe that the things which we had seen with our own eyes and heard with our own ears were living truths. Every trace of all that had been blotted out. The castle stood as before, reared high above a waste of desolation.

When we got home, we were talking of the old time, which we could all look back on without despair. I took the papers from the safe where they had been ever since our return so long ago. We were struck with the fact, that in all the mass of material of which the record is composed, there is hardly one authentic document: nothing but a mass of typewriting, except the later notebooks of Mina and Seward and myself, and Van Helsing's memorandum. We could hardly ask anyone, even did we wish to, to accept these as proofs of so wild a story.'

JONATHAN HARKER – Extract from his journal of 1894

1

LIFEBLOOD

I have to admit. In glancing over the incoherent series of memoirs with which I, Dr. John Watson, have endeavored to illustrate a few of the mental peculiarities of my good friend and companion, Mr. Sherlock Holmes, I am struck by the difficulty which I experienced in picking out examples which shall in every way answer my purpose. For in those cases in which Holmes has performed some splendid conquest of analytical deduction and has showed the value of his peculiar methods of investigation, the facts themselves have often been so slight or so commonplace that I could not feel justified in laying them before the public.

It has frequently happened that Holmes has been concerned in some research where the facts have been of the most remarkable and dramatic character, but where the share which he has himself taken in determining their causes has been less pronounced than I, as his biographer, could wish.

The events which form this account are of such a blur that it is difficult to recount that they span seven years, erupting to finality in the same count of days. A week that pushed us both to the limit of human belief and understanding, a limit that we have determined to have no part in revisiting for the rest of our time on this earth. I cannot underestimate the horror of those gloomy days. They will remain with us for all time.

Maybe in the business of which I am now about to write, I have not stressed the part which my friend played enough. Yet the entire train of circumstances is so remarkable that I cannot bring myself to omit it entirely. To assist in the consideration of this case, the reader may warrant having at hand the journals relating to Dracula as transcribed to type by Mina Harker. The accounts of that time are, in themselves, eternal and relevant to the day that you may read my report, and useful should you ever become part of such a series of events. The likes of which hang over us all during the hours of darkness.

2

ARRIVAL OF THE GHOST SHIP

The morning of Monday of August 8, 1887, had started some hours ago, carrying upon it the uncommon clear brilliance of a late autumn sky. For once the common shroud of fog and dank air of London town had dispersed, if only for a few hours. Nevertheless, the interior of the flat at 221B Baker Street remained in darkness.

I made my way to the window that faced the thoroughfare and tugged at the drawn curtains with both hands. The act establishing a narrow opening in the heavy material as the drapes scratched across their runners. The daylight encroached. Delivering with it a pinhole view of the activities on the street below. Taken through scrunched eyes as they adjusted to the delivery of such brightness.

I observed the owner of the general store to the left of our accommodation, Janssen the cheese monger. He was scurrying about the frontage of his shop, putting out a selection of his delicious goods into prime view. Hoping to lure passersby to a purchase that they had yet no plan to make. As he arranged them for best display it crossed my mind, he was wasting his effort. Even though it was a perfect day to do so. His cheeses sold more by reputation and taste rather than by appearance. Those cloth wound bundles having no more aesthetic value than a beekeeper's hat. His sales greatly assisted by the short supply of good cheeses now running throughout the nation.

My opinion of the matter, for I was no cheese salesperson, was doubtless of little value. Indeed, who was I to instruct an expert in the way of his business, as I knew very well from my dealings with Sherlock.

I turned inward to the room. Through the gap in the

curtains the beam of sharp morning light cut into the unclear bloom, displaying a dense sprinkling of speckles, dancing as they carried in the air. Each hanging, then glittering like a fairy, just for a moment caught in the streaming sunlight. I stood close to the armchair Sherlock used when interviewing clients. Its worn leather had witnessed many intriguing tales.

To its right, a tall wooden rack that acted as a repository for his pipe, which was at this moment in Sherlock's hands. The wide mantle above the open fire held various trinkets, together with the clock that beat out time, with no regard to its duty to delay in times of urgency. I carried a few steps to the breakfast table that lay in front of me, and at which Sherlock sat in thought. The exhaust from his tobacco laden pipe rising to join with the melancholy of the gloom to which it contributed. Picking up the Sunday newspaper that lay beside the breakfast in front of him, I read to myself. The article of the main headline a striking title, I thought.

"Well, I say Holmes. Look here, the arrival of a ghost ship!"

Sherlock made no return. Clearing my throat to establish

a hint of melodrama, then momentarily flapping the pages of the Westminster Gazette before me like the wings of a giant bird. I read again the title, declaring with a stronger volume, and reiterating.

“Hum! Hum! There is an arrival of a ghost ship. In Whitby no less!”

Sherlock remained steadfast, leaning over the table, his chin supported by his hands set above his elbows as they formed a triangle upon the top. His pipe releasing the last wisp of its combustion into the air. His position was a common one of most recent mornings. Unflinching and rather morose, the look completed with silk dressing gown and leather slippers, having only just arisen for the day. In front of him, a breakfast prepared by Mrs. Hudson. Two hard-boiled eggs sitting comfortably in their cups and toast in its rack, all untouched and cold. Leaning against the rack, a piece of correspondence, Sherlock’s eyes set firmly upon the envelope.

I glanced at the clock on the mantle. It was ten thirty-five. He was as a statue, making no response or movement other than a rhythmic puff of his exhausted pipe, which suddenly emitted a strange whistle on his draw. I presume the high pitch called dogs from some distance. I commenced my reading aloud from the article in the

Gazette. Determined, he would find interest in the descriptive words of the journalist who had reported the affair.

"On the night of Saturday, August 6th, 1887, I became witness to one of the greatest and strangest of storms on record off the east coast of Whitby. The results of which were both dark and terrifying, and still hang over my thoughts like the clouds and the remarkable message that was delivered by a shipwreck that night. I am uncertain that I will ever sleep without disturbance again."

"The storm itself appearing with no official notice from an unusually fine day. Initially, the wind was blowing mildly from the south-west, with no concern being raised by the coastguard. However, William Gregg, a crab fisher of these seas for fifty years, came scurrying towards me, carried on legs buckled through arthritic knees, his brow furrowed upon his sea-weathered face. He foretold insistently the coming of a sudden and heavy storm. 'Mark my words, the devil is in the sky this evening.' He said, his voice cracking with fear as he pointed with a bent finger towards the sky."

"It would be hard to fathom that this could be true, as the

approach of sunset was so exquisite, so grand in its masses of splendidly colored clouds, that such a change would be possible at all. Before the sun dipped below the black mass of Kettleness, standing boldly across the western sky, its decent was above a mixture of clouds of every sunset-color. Flame red, purple, pink, green, violet, and all the tints of gold and amber; with here and there masses not large, but of absolute blackness, in many shapes, as well outlined as colossal silhouettes.

The night assumed its place and at nine o'clock there was a dead calm over the sea, the waning brightness of the moon, sharing the sultry heat by its illumination, bringing with it a distant rolling thunder, echoing from the horizon and through the bay."

"In the distance, the only sail noticeable, raised upon a foreign schooner. The boat going westwards into the darkness of the approaching storm. Now, realizing the danger, the coastguard made many efforts to signal for the vessel to reduce sail. Before the black clouds covered the glare of the moon, we saw the ship with sails idly flapping as it rolled on the undulating swell of the sea. A little after midnight came a strange sound, and high overhead the air carried a strange, faint, hollow booming, that sounded unlike any thunder heard by human ear."

"Without warning, the storm broke upon the calmness of the gentle seas. Nature at once became convulsed. The waves rose in growing fury, each overtopping its fellow. Until in a very few minutes the lately glassy sea was like a roaring monster. The white-crested waves beat madly on the level sands and rushed up the shelving cliffs; others broke over the pier of Whitby Harbor. The turmoil brought with it masses of thick sea-fog of a strange ochre hew.

Drifting inland, the white, wet clouds, which swept by in ghostly fashion, so dank and cold that it needed but little effort of imagination to think that the spirits of those lost at sea were touching their living brethren with the clammy hands of death. Sporadically, the mist cleared, and in the openings, we could see the raging sea in the lightning's glare, which now came thick and fast. The disturbance followed by such sudden peals of thunder that the entire sky overhead seemed trembling under the shock of the progression of the storm."

"On the summit of the East Cliff, the searchlight panning the horizon like the sweep of a sharp blade, discovered some distance away the schooner. The same vessel noticed earlier in the evening. The wind had by this time turned opposite and backed to the east. Between the boat and the port, lay the great flat reef on which so many splendid ships have from time to time suffered. With the wind blowing from its present quarter, it would be quite impossible that she should fetch the entrance of the harbor.

It was now nearly the hour of high tide, but the waves were so great that in their troughs the shallows of the shore were almost visible, and the schooner, with all sails set, was rushing with such speed that, in the words William Gregg, 'she must fetch up somewhere, if it be only in hell.'"

"Then came another deluge of sea-fog, greater than any that led before it, a mass of dank mist, which seemed to close on all things like a yellowy-grey pall. They kept the piercing beam of the searchlight fixed on the harbor mouth across the East Pier, where the boat was being led. The onlookers waited breathlessly. The wind suddenly shifted to the north-east, and the remnant of the sea-fog melted in the blast; and then, in ultimate wonder, between the piers, leaping from wave to wave as it rushed at headlong speed, swept the strange schooner taken by the blast, with all sail set, gaining the safety of the harbor."

"The searchlight followed the boat. A shudder ran through all who saw, for lashed to the helm was a corpse, with drooping head, which swung horribly back and forth at each motion of the ship. I could see no other form on deck at all. The schooner did not slow but rushed across the harbor. Finally pitching upon on the accumulation of sand and gravel washed by many tides and many storms into the south-east corner of the pier jutting under the East Cliff, known locally as Tate Hill Pier."

"There was of course a considerable concussion as the vessel drove up on the sand heap. Every spar, rope, and stay strained. The top-hammer of the mast came crashing down. But, strangest of all, the very instant the boat touched shore, an immense dog sprang up on deck from below, as if shot up by the impact. The dog jumped from the bow on the sand. It made straight for the steep cliff, where the churchyard hangs over the laneway to the East Pier so steeply that some of the flat tombstone's project over where the sustaining cliff has fallen away. The animal disappeared in the darkness, which seemed intensified just beyond the focus of the searchlight."

"When I arrived at the wreck, I could climb on deck, and was one of a small group who saw the dead sailor still lashed to the wheel. The man fastened only by his hands, tied one over the other, to a spoke of the wheel. Held securely between the inner hand and the wood was a crucifix. The set of beads on which it hung, being around both wrists and wheel, and all kept fast by the binding cords. The poor fellow seated at one time. But the thrashing and buffeting of the sails had worked through the rudder of the wheel and dragged him back and forth, so that the fibers with which they tied him had cut the flesh to the bone."

"Shortly after, under a red sky, the storm subsided, the crowds scattered, and all was serene. I shall report further details of the derelict ship, known as 'THE DEMETER', which found her way so miraculously into harbor in the storm in a following edition of this paper." I rested for a moment, with no attention being made by Sherlock. I asked.

"A quite remarkable article, you suppose Sherlock. Do you think there is anything to it?"

I folded the copy of the Gazette back into its form and deposited it firmly in front of the teapot, whence it first came into my hand. The twin boiled eggs rattling in their cups and the toast in its rack. Sherlock, remaining unmoved by my rendition of a purported mystery, said dismissively.

"My dear Watson, such scandal of weather and wreck is easily reported by journalists seeking to be the next fashion."

Sherlock, somewhat distracted, played with the correspondence taken from its position, rotating it between his fingers. He had it already opened.

3

THE LETTER

"I am prompted to think...," said I.

"I should do so," Sherlock Holmes remarked impatiently.

I believe I am one of the most long-suffering of mortals; but I will admit that the disdainful interruption annoyed me. "Really, Holmes," said I firmly, "you are a little irritating."

He was too much absorbed with his own thoughts to give any immediate answer to my remonstrance. He leaned again upon a single hand, with his untasted breakfast before him, and he stared at the slip of paper which he had drawn from its envelope. Then he took the envelope itself, held it up to the shaft of light now penetrating the room, and thoroughly studied both the exterior and the flap.

"It is his writing," said he thoughtfully. "I can hardly doubt that it is Harker's writing, though I have seen it only twice before. The Spencerian 'y' with the peculiar under arch and embellishment is distinctive. But if it is Harker, thus it must be the very first importance."

He was speaking to himself rather than to me; but my vexation disappeared in the interest of which the words awakened.

"Who again is Harker?" I asked.

"Harker. Watson is a man whose life, if it lay not his entire spirit in turmoil. A name with nothing but a walking shell to hold it; but behind lies a resilient and remarkable personality. In a former letter he frankly informed me that his life was not his own and defied me ever to trace him among the teeming millions of this great city if he was fortunate to ever return to these shores. Harker is noteworthy, not for himself, but for the great man with whom he is in touch. Picture to yourself the pilot fish with the shark, the jackal with the lion, anything that is insignificant in companionship with what is formidable: not only formidable, Watson, but malevolent, in the loftiest degree sinister. That is where he comes within my domain. You have heard me tell of Count Dracula?"

"The peculiar if not fictional embodiment of evil, as famous as any superstition as..."

"Such superstition, Watson." Holmes murmured in a deprecating tone.

"I was about to say, as the public know him."

"A touch! A distinct touch!" cried Holmes. "You are gaining a certain unexpected vein of gawky humor, Watson, against which I must learn to guard myself. But in calling Dracula a fictional embodiment of evil you are uttering libel in the eyes of the shadowy underworld to which he is attached. There lie the majesty and the spectacle of it! The greatest evil of all time, the designer of every deviltry, the controlling intellect of the under-spirit-world, an intellect which might have made or marred the destiny of nations, that is the creature!"

"But so aloof is he from general suspicion, so immune from criticism, so exquisite in his management and self-effacement, that for those very words that you have uttered he could visit you with a meeting, of his time and choosing, holding himself under the cloak of darkness to emerge with your life essence in payment for his injured character. Is he not the legend that lays within a box of dirt in a castle somewhere in the Carpathian Mountains? Is this a man to denigrate? Innocent doctor and vengeful Count, such would be your respective roles! That is brilliance, Watson. But if I am spared by lesser men, our day will assuredly come."

"May I be there to see!" I exclaimed devoutly. "But you were speaking of this man Harker."

"Ah, yes, Harker is a link in the chain some little way from its great attachment. Harker is not quite a sound link, between us. He is the only flaw in that chain so far as I have been able to test it."

"But no chain is stronger than its weakest link."

"Exactly, my dear Watson! Hence the exaggerated importance of Harker. Led on by some rudimentary aspirations towards good and encouraged by the judicious stimulation of a desire to defeat this evil before the beloved that he holds dear are told to suffer. He has once given me advance information which has been of value, that highest value which expects and prevents rather than avenges the deviousness against the spirt of humankind."

Holmes flattened out the paper with the back part of both hands to avoid contamination with sweat or grease. A letter. Correspondence in Harker's hand addressed to Mr. SH., London, and dated June 29, using the care of address 221B Baker Street. I rose and, leaning over him, stared down at the contents, which also contained a peculiar inscription, almost invisible at the bottom of the page, which ran:

29 June 1887

Dear Sir,

I write in hope that this message finds you well. I am expecting to return to London within the next few weeks and upon my arrival I should solicit your council. In a place and at a time I will show upon my landfall.

Yours with respect

JONATHAN HARKER.

The inscription followed:

PURFLEET, 7-5-1938, 4-5-12, 8-5-466. SEWARD, 29-6-58,

IN, 29-6-137. 5-5-372, NOT, 5-5-2. 4-5-344, WHITBY.

“What do you make of it, Holmes?”

“It is plainly an attempt to convey a secret message.”

“But what is the use of a cipher message without the cipher?”

“In this instance, none.”

“Why do you say, ‘in this instance’?”

“Because there are many ciphers which I would read as easily as I do the mused content of the agony column: such crude devices amuse the intelligence without fatiguing it. But this is different. It is clearly a reference to the words on a page, or pages of some book. Until I am told which book, I am powerless.”

“WHITBY is, I would offer self-explanatory, being the town in the north-east, the same town as I read just now joining the article. But why ‘SEWARD’ and ‘PURFLEET’?”

“Clearly because those are words which were not contained in the page in question. What article Watson?”

"Then why has he not showed the book? And coincidence by chance Holmes, the article, the ghost ship, run aground in Whitby!"

"Whitby, yes that strikes me odd if not a coincidence, as you put it, as there are none known to man but in his imagination. However, your native shrewdness, my dear Watson, that instinctive cunning which is the delight of your acquaintances, would surely prevent you from enclosing cipher and message in the same envelope. Should it miscarry, you are undone. As it is, both must go wrong before any harm comes from it. Our second post is now overdue, and I shall be surprised if it does not bring us either a further letter of explanation, or as is more probable, the very volume to which these figures refer."

The appearance of Billy, the postal delivery boy fulfilled within a very few minutes after Holmes's calculation, with the very correspondence which we were expecting.

"The same writing, just about," remarked Holmes, as he opened the envelope, "and noted to be a further missive of one Jonathan Harker," he added in an exultant voice as he unfolded the letter. "Come, we are getting on, Watson." His brow clouded, however, as he glanced over the contents.

"Dear me, this is very disconcerting! I fear, Watson, that all our expectations come to nothing. I trust that the man Harker will come to no harm."

"What expresses the correspondence Holmes?"

"It is dated June 30, 1887" Sherlock handed me the letter. I found the writing to be more like scribble and, as such, it was harder to read.

Dear Sir,

I will go no further in this matter. It is too dangerous; he suspects me. I can see that he suspects me. He came to me unexpectedly the preceding night. After I had addressed the envelope containing the cipher. I could cover it up. If he had seen it, it would have gone hard with me. But I read suspicion in his eyes, those hypnotic, peculiar eyes. Please burn the cipher message, which can now be of no use to you. I am holding my journal and will deliver that should it prove to be a possibility as he will arrive in England himself.

Yours.

JONATHAN HARKER.

Holmes sat for some little time, twisting this letter between his fingers, and frowning, as he stared into the fire. Its flames playing with the rear of the hearth in which it sat and creating columns of glowing orange embers that stuck like redcoats to the chimney back. He considered the plea in the letter to burn the message but decided that moment to apply its contents to his reasoning, to resolve the conundrum which it posed.

"After all," he said at last, "there maybe nothing in it. It may be only his guilty conscience. Knowing himself to be a traitor, he may have read the accusation in the other's eyes."

"The other being, I presume, Count Dracula."

"No less! When any of that party talk about 'He' you know whom they mean. There is one predominant 'He' for all of them."

"But what can 'He' do?"

"Hum! That is a question of considerable magnitude. When you have one of the most devious of brains of Europe up against you, and all the powers of darkness at his back, there are infinite possibilities. Anyhow, my friend Harker is evidently scared out of his senses. Kindly compare the writing in the note to that upon the previous letter, which was done only a day before this ill-omened correspondence. The one is clear and firm. The other hardly legible. Nothing more than a scrawl."

"Why did he write at all? Why did he not simply drop it?"

"Because he feared I would make some inquiry after him in that case, and possibly bring trouble on him. That and the fact of the arrival in England of the Count prior to Harker himself."

"The arrival of the Count?" said I. "Of course." Sherlock returned.

I had picked up the original cipher message and was bending my brows over it. "It's pretty maddening to think that an important secret may lie here on this slip of paper, and that it is beyond human power to penetrate it." I pulled a spare paper to the table and sketched upon it the cipher, now in larger characters, so it would be easier to read.

Sherlock Holmes had pushed away his untried breakfast and lit the familiar unsavory pipe which was the companion of his deepest meditations. "I wonder!" said he, leaning back and staring at the ceiling. "Perhaps there are points which have escaped your Machiavellian intellect. Let us consider the problem in the light of pure reason. This man's reference is to a journal. That is our point of departure."

"A somewhat vague one."

"Let us see then if we can narrow it down. As I focus my mind upon it, it seems rather less impenetrable. What indications have we as to the whereabouts of this book?"

"None."

"So there belongs the challenge, my good doctor. We need to seek the book."

4

THE CIPHER REVIVED

Seven years and several months had passed between today's date, Monday October 29th, 1894, and the fateful day of arrival of the ghost ship in Whitby. The same moment that had brought the delivery of the coded letter from Harker to Baker Street. Sherlock and I had investigated many cases in between, but none would match the one that I am about to tell now. One which starts at the delivery of Harker's coded correspondence and sets further with an unannounced visitor.

The month was leaving us with a passage of exceptional violence, in rain and cold. The fogs had increased in intensity and color, with the dense air holding them tight as a blanket to the ground. They were no doubt leading us towards another bleak winter, one in a long sequence of others.

All day the wind had howled like a wolf, and the rain had beaten against the cold glass of the windows. So much, that even here in the core of great, human-made London we were forced to raise our minds for the instant from the routine of life and to recognize those great elemental forces which shriek at humanity through the bars of his civilization, like untamed beasts in a cage. As evening drew in, the storm grew greater and rowdier, and the wind wailed and whimpered like a child in the chimney.

The darkness tightened around the bleak edges of buildings. Pushing citizens still on the streets, towards their home and shelter. If they were lucky enough to have one. Sherlock Holmes sat moodily at one side of the fireplace cross-indexing his records of crime, while I at the other was deep in one of Clark Russell's great sea-stories until the moan of the gale from without seemed to meld with the text, and the splash of the rain to expand out into the deep rhythmic swash of the ocean waves.

"Why," said I, glancing up at my colleague, "that was surely a knock at the door. Who could come to-night? Some friend of yours, perhaps?"

"Except yourself I have none," he answered. "I do not encourage visitors."

"A client, then?"

"If so, it is a serious case. Nothing less would bring a man or woman out on such a day and at such an hour. But I would postulate that it is more likely to be some crony of our landlady, the affable Mrs. Hudson."

For once, Sherlock Holmes was half wrong in his conjecture, however, for there came a step in the passage and a tapping at the door. A quiet, hesitant knock. He stretched out his long arm to turn the lamp away from himself and towards the vacant chair upon which a newcomer must sit.

"Come in!" said he.

The woman who entered was young, some seven-and-twenty at the outside, well dressed and trimly clad, with something of refinement and delicacy in her bearing. The streaming umbrella which she held in her hand, and her long shining waterproof, told of the fierce weather through which she had come. She carried with her a medium-sized carpet bag, being made from a brightly patterned oriental rug, which she held tightly under her arm.

"Mr. Holmes, I owe you an apology," she said, dropping the bag under its own weight and removing one of her white leather gloves, then the other, pinching the fingertips, one after the other, before pulling gently at them. "I trust I am not intruding. I fear that I have brought some traces of the storm and rain into your snug chamber." Her hands were as pale as her complexion, the skin carrying a greater translucency than I would expect. Even with exposure to the bleak air. She presented to my eyes as possessing an anemia.

"Give me your coat and umbrella," said Holmes. "They may rest here on the hook and will be dry presently. Please, sit yourself in the chair and enjoy the fire while you inform us of your intent tonight. You have come down from the north-east, I see."

She looked about anxiously in the lamp's glare, and I could see that her face was pale and her eyes heavy, like those of a woman who weighed down with some great anxiety. She seemed somewhat distant in her thought, and it surprised me she answered with a quick return.

"Yes, from Whitby." She said, still catching her breath. "How, do you know that?"

"That fine sand, clay and shale mixture which I see upon the heels of your boots is quite distinctive. Most likely from the area of the harbor, or the path that leads to the Abbey above." Sherlock said, sitting further back in his chair, satisfied that he had already engaged his mind towards the mystery that would soon appear.

"Your keen eye and your instinctive detective nature are why I am here. I have come for advice, to deliver a package and ask for help."

"Advice is easily got; a package quickly deposited, but help is not always so easy."

"I have heard of you, Mr. Holmes. I know from Jonathan how he corresponded in secret to this address when he was held at the castle those years ago."

"Jonathan. Mr. Harker? You know of him. He is well then and back in England?"

"Why yes Mr. Holmes, I am his wife Mina. We married upon his return to these shores, although he remains fragile in health."

"He said that you could solve anything."

"He said too much."

"That you are never beaten."

"I have been beaten four times, three times by men, and once by a woman."

"But what is that compared with the number of your successes?"

"It is true that I have been generally successful."

"Then you may be so with me."

"I beg you will draw your chair closer to the fire and favor me with some details as to the information that you are here to deliver. I wish to hear more of the adventures of your husband, Mrs. Harker. The last I know of his situation was when, as you say, he was held as a prisoner by Count Dracula, seven years since."

"Yes, he was a prisoner there and suffered greatly. The details of the issue are many. It is no simple one."

"None of those which come to me are. I am the last court of appeal."

"And yet I question, sir, whether, in all your experience, you have ever listened to a more inexplicable chain of events than those which have happened and which I bring now to your scrutiny."

"You fill me with interest," said Holmes. "Pray deliver us the fundamental facts from the commencement, and I can then question you as to those details which seem to me to be most important."

The young woman pulled up her chair closer to the fire, pushing her wet feet out towards the blaze, the steam from the heated white leather of her boots rising into the air above them.

"My name," said she, "as you now know, is Mina. To give you an idea of the facts, I must go back to the outset of the matter."

"That is commonly the best place to find the start." Said Holmes.

5

THE SIREN ARRIVES

The young woman sat in silence for a moment. The convex mirrors of the cornea of her unflinching eyes reflecting the flickering light of the flames in front of her. Holmes and I waited for her description; it came from her as a rush and with hardly a breath:

"It was mid-August, seven years ago now, not soon after midnight. I was sharing a room with my good friend Lucy. That night, without reason that I knew of, she left her bed and walked out of the house. I looked for her and eventually saw her, hunched on a bench in the churchyard. A man I first assumed, but not one that I had seen before, stood over her. The face was white, set within it a deep red in his gleaming eyes. The figure bent over her as she lay. When I ran to be with her, the man had disappeared. I know now that was him. She was still, breathing in a shallow response, alone and asleep. I woke her as from a dream, for she had a confusion about her face, we returned home without further conversation."

"By 'him' to mean Dracula?" I asked.

"Yes, it was him!" Mina continued.

"It filled me with apprehension about Lucy, not merely for her health, lest she should suffer from the exposure to the chilly night, but for her reputation in case the story should get into the fickle hands of the village gossip. After we returned to the house, cleaned our feet from the muck of the path, we said a prayer of thankfulness together. I tucked her into bed. Before falling asleep she asked, even implored, me not to report a word to anybody, not even her mother, about her sleep-walking adventure. I locked the door and tied the key to my wrist. Lucy was sleeping soundly."

"My word Holmes, what is to do here." Said I.

“Let the lady finish. I perceive she has much more to say.”

“Yes, my good sirs. There is much more about this than I have presently expounded.”

Mina carried on; her eyes still affixed to the flames of the fire, as if in a hypnotic state.

“The next morning, I had breakfast as normal. Lucy was still sleeping, and she remained so till I woke her and seemed not to have even changed her side, remaining in the same position as I had left her. The adventure of the night had not seemed to have harmed her; It had benefited her, for she looked better that morning than she had done for weeks. It was then I noticed; the skin of her throat pierced. I thought I must have pinched up a piece of relaxed skin and have transfixed it with a pin I applied to fix her shawl the night before, for there were two little red points like pinpricks, and on the band of her nightdress was a drop of blood. I apologized and became troubled about it. She giggled and replied she did not even feel it. Fortunately, it cannot leave a scar, as it is so minuscule.”

“Two nights hence I awoke to find Lucy standing against the window. I moved between her and the glass, to find, flitting between me and the moonlight, a great bat, coming and going in great whirling circles. Once or twice, it came quite close, but was, I suppose, frightened at seeing me, and flitted away across the harbor towards the abbey. When I came back from the window Lucy had lain down again and was sleeping peacefully. She stirred and spoke without waking 'his red eyes again! They are just the same.' It was such an odd expression."

"I awoke later and there distinctly was Lucy with her head lying up against the side of the windowsill and her eyes shut. She was fast asleep, and by her, seated on the windowsill, was something that looked like a good-sized bird. As I motioned to get out of bed she moved back to her bed, fell fast asleep, panting; she was holding her hand to her throat, as though to protect it from cold."

"Over the next few days Lucy grew weaker and more languid. I did not understand her fading away as she was doing. She ate and slept well and enjoyed the fresh air; but all the time the roses in her cheeks were fading. At night I could hear her gasping as if for air. I kept the key to our door always fastened to my wrist at night, but she gets up and wanders about the room, and sits at the open window. One night I found her leaning out when I woke up, and when I tried to wake her, I could not; she was in a faint."

"When I looked at her throat as she lay asleep, the tiny wounds seem not to have healed. They were still open, and larger than before, and the edges of them were faintly white. They were like little white dots with red centers. I thought that the doctor should see them."

"My dear lady, perhaps you should break for a moment as you have been delivering the tale for some good few minutes." Said I.

"No, it is best if the complete account is told as I recall from start to finish, lest I overlook some essential matter to it."

Mina continued without further hesitation.

"It was around this time, as we learned later, several wooden boxes found on the ghost ship, landed more than a week before in Whitby, were to be transported to an estate in London."

"The ghost ship, Holmes!"

"Quite so, Watson. Please continue Mina."

"It was a few days more, around the second week in August, I received news from Mr. Hawkins, Jonathan's employer, that Jonathan was extremely ill in the hospital in Buda-Pesth. Receiving treatment for a violent brain fever, he had been there for six weeks. I travelled to Hull, and caught the boat to Hamburg, and then the train to Buda-Pesth."

"When I arrived at the hospital, I found Jonathan was so thin, pale, and weak looking. His spirit defeated. All the resolution had flown out of his dear lifeless eyes. He was only a wreck of himself, and he did not remember all that had happened to him for a long time later."

"We returned to London rather than our home in Whitby; there we met Professor Van Helsing through Dr. Seward, who was at the time treating Lucy for her maladies. Van Helsing seemed to understand the reasons for her malady and applied treatments to her before returning to Amsterdam. For a while she seemed to recover. He provided medicines to place in her window and around her neck. But then in mid-September misfortunes hit. First the sudden death of Mr. Hawkins, and then of Lucy's mother. Lucy herself died only a few days later."

"That is when the most remarkable thing occurred. As we sat in a café in London, Jonathan became very disturbed. I asked him why so? He answered, evidently thinking that I knew as much about it as he did. He informed me he had seen the Count pass-by. Crying out that Dracula had grown so young."

"Later that month, Professor Van Helsing visited with some urgency on the news that the Count was in London. We found Dracula had used a London estate. We, including Van Helsing, tracked him, and finally back to his lair in Transylvania. There we thought we had destroyed him. However, from recent articles in the Westminster Gazette he may be back in town, impossible as that seems."

"A remarkable story, Mrs. Harker. You said that you had a package to deliver?"

She reached to her carpetbag at her feet and removed a large brown paper parcel.

"Gentlemen, here is Jonathan's journal, notes and other documents that I have recorded, through typewritten copy, made some time ago. You may examine them all."

"I say Holmes! The journal!" Said I with an excitement.

"Before we discover the contents of the journal that you deliver, please tell me more of this man, Van Helsing. I presume one of the primary concerns of your visit?" Said Holmes.

"Professor Van Helsing is the man about this matter that saved us all. And is the reason that I approach you now. But, how did you know that Van Helsing was one of my reasons for being here tonight?"

"Yes, how so, Holmes?" I added.

"It must have been that some success had been at the expense of the Count, and this success was because of the intervention and advice of Van Helsing, and to a lesser extent, of the other companions. Over three and less than six, I calculate."

"Yes Mr. Holmes, you are correct. The team that assembled to deliver the world from the evil of this Count comprised five. They were Jonathan, Professor Van Helsing, Lord Godalming, Dr. Seward and Mr. Quincey Morris."

"And you, Mrs. Harker, and you." Said Sherlock.

6

JONATHAN'S JOURNAL

The brown wax paper wrapped expertly around the journals had preserved them effectively from the wind and rain. Struggling to extract the several knots that held the coarse string tight around the bundle, I eventually opened the seal to release the contents. The journals and other papers fell into my hands. I held them steady and removed what I hoped would be Harker's journal. I was correct, the heaviest of the set. The first page blank, save the title: 'JOURNAL OF JONATHAN HARKER.' For its size it was a weighty book, at least one-hundred and fifty pages, with over three quarters filled with handwriting, but not entirely legible. The journal had its duplicate, a typed copy carefully transcribed by Mina. I shall enter the complete document, and its partners, into the record of these events as appendices to this account as their contents are miraculous and disturbing at the same time and form the story from its beginning. Within them are details that set out the foundation towards many of the findings that we would shortly discover.

“Mina. If I may address you as such?”

“Yes, Mr. Holmes, you may.”

“Thank you. In return you shall address me as Sherlock. Now we have settled that, please, in your own thoughts, recap the contents, save us all reading the entirety of Jonathan’s journal.”

“Yes, I may do that. The date was May of the year, seven years prior to this one. It had been a pleasant spring and Jonathan was excited about embarking to Europe for his assignment. I set him on his path. I knew I would miss him dearly. The purpose of his project meant that he was to venture to Transylvania, somewhere remote in the Carpathian Mountains, to undertake a business charter with the man that we now know to be the Count. The locals at the tavern where he first stayed, before he began his travels to the castle where the Count lived, solicited to change his mind about continuing. It troubled him as he witnessed their dread. Before leaving on the coach, as arranged. We all wish now that he had heeded their forewarnings, for the warnings were far gentler that the reality that he would soon endure."

Mina stopped for a moment as she seemed to recall the occasion that Jonathan's fate, together with her own, was sealed.

"This is the first warning of the fear that gripped all those around him, like a bulky woolen overcoat. On completing his transfer to the castle, he met Dracula, first as a tall old man, clean shaven save for a long white moustache, and clad in black from head to foot, without a single speck of color about him anywhere, neither on his clothing or in his flesh. We now know that his appearance may change from time to time, but to Jonathan, that was the Count's form at the beginning."

"Jonathan learned that the Count had saturated himself in the study of all about England and had the idea to venture there. He held within the castle a great number of books, entire shelves full of them, and bound volumes of magazines and newspapers of the most varied kind.

History, geography, politics, political economy, botany, geology, law, all relating to England and English life and customs and manners."

"One book was an atlas. Upon viewing, Jonathan found in specific places three little circles drawn carefully and marked precisely with ink. On inspection he noticed one was near London on the eastside, manifestly where the Count's new estate was situated; of the other two one was in Exeter, in the southwest, and the Whitby on the northeast Yorkshire coast, his home."

"It was not before a few days had passed that Jonathan witnessed several strange and quite remarkable events. Too many to recount before reciting the journal in entirety, which would have no place here, not. In one instance, which he found to be unbelieving of his own eyes, Jonathan found the Count issued no reflection, neither in the mirror nor glass. There were other behaviors that he noticed; that Dracula attracted to blood and repulsed by the crucifix. It was also that my poor Jonathan became aware, but too late, that he was a prisoner in the castle and Dracula had no intention of releasing him without harm. In time, the Count discussed various business dealings that he wished to conduct within England. One regarding the carrying of cargo to an English port and thereafter transported to his estate."

"Do you think that would be Whitby, Holmes?" I interrupted.

"A precocious connection you make, Watson, but maybe closer to the fact of the matter than we have yet to discover." Mina continued.

"There was no end to the imprisonment and the following nights became more and more horrific, filled with apparitions that could not readily be explained. Jonathan describes in his journal the moment that he witnessed Dracula slowly emerge from a castle window and crawl down the castle wall. The claw-like hands allowed him to travel face down, with his cloak spreading out around him like great wings, defying gravity."

"Is there any sign of what the Count's business was further about?" Asked Sherlock.

"The Count compelled Jonathan to write letters. Each composed by the Count himself. Jonathan smuggled others to the outside world."

"The correspondence to you, I think Holmes. Pardon my interruption." Said I.

"Precisely, my dear Watson. Please continue Mina."

"There were many additional letters that the Count found and destroyed, although not those that contained the cipher of certain things that are forecast to be true, and which Jonathan had overheard in planning."

"Jonathan made the discovery of one of the fifty boxes that were held in the castle to be transported, within a pile of newly dug earth, laid as to sleep was the Count. Jonathan set out his escape. I am uncertain how he did, but he appeared deposited by others at the hospital. When I found him, he did not fully realize that he was still alive. I fetched him back home, in a terrible state from which he is still suffering. Each night he hallucinates and speaks in conversation."

"Good Lord! Holmes, the man, considered he was lost! And what of this narrative?"

"We recognize there is more to it, Watson."

"Yes, there is much more to this, my honorable gentlemen." Said Mina.

7

THE MESSAGE DECIPHERED

"Now Watson, pull the letter and the cipher from the file."

I sought from the dusty and unordered bookshelf the file labelled Harker and pulled the letter, together with the note that I had made of the coded message, blowing off the dust as I did so. An anomaly which often struck me in the character of my friend Sherlock Holmes was that, although in his methods of thought he was the neatest and most methodical of humanity. He always affected a certain quiet primness of dress. Holmes was none the less in his personal habits than one of the untidiest men that ever drove a fellow-lodger to distraction. Not that I am in the least conventional in that respect myself. The rough-and-tumble work in Afghanistan, coming on the top of a natural Bohemianism of disposition, has made me rather laxer than befits a medical man. But with me there is a limit, and when I find a man who keeps his cigars in the coal scuttle, his tobacco in the toe end of a worn Persian slipper, and his unanswered correspondence transfixed by a letter knife into the very center of his wooden mantelpiece, then I give myself virtuous airs. I have always held, too, that pistol practice should be distinctly an open-air pastime; and when Holmes, in one of his self-centered humors, would sit in an armchair with his hair-trigger and a hundred cartridges, and adorn the opposite wall with bullet holes, I felt strongly that neither the atmosphere nor the appearance of our room improved by it.

“Sherlock, you really must allow Mrs. Hudson to dust this place.” Said I.

“Watson, dust is often more the friend of the detective than the bullet or the knife.” Sherlock replied.

I took the paper with the cipher and read it aloud.

"PURFLEET, 7-5-1938, 4-5-12, 8-5-466. SEWARD, 29-6-58, IN, 29-6-137. 5-5-372, NOT, 5-5-2. 4-5-344, WHITBY."

"Well, well, it is surely not so bad as we thought. Let us first put the words contained to one side. The cipher message then begins with a 7, does it not? We may take it as a working hypothesis that 7 is the particular page or paragraph to which the cipher refers. So, our cipher has already taken a shape, which is surely something gained. What other indications have we as to this journal? The next number is 5. What do you make of that, Watson?"

"The seventh chapter, fifth page, no doubt."

"Possibly, but in this case, hardly so, Watson. You will, I am sure, agree with me that if the page be given, the number of the chapter is immaterial. Also, observe that the journal does not contain chapters, but sections started with a particular date. You know my methods in such cases, Watson. I put myself in the man's place and, having first gauged his intelligence, I try to imagine how I should myself have proceeded under the same circumstances."

The heavy book lay open in my hands. Its leather binding warming to the touch. I flicked once through its many pages from front to back and then in return from back to front like I would to the edge of a deck of cards. I glimpsed the parts of the pages as they passed in front of each other. The writing was all by the same hand, in some sort of scribble, although its neatness reduced as the volume progressed. Holmes was correct. There were no chapters, but sections named by the date to which Jonathan wrote them, more like a diary. I fell on the last page.

"Death did not find the fellow, as he imagined it would, eh?"

"I think we are aware of the situation, Watson. Please continue with the cipher. Now you have studied it in your hands, let us apply the first part of the code, 7-5-1938, so what of the 1938?"

"The journal is not comprehensible as writing Holmes, other than the dates which start the sections, I would form a guess, that it is also a cipher."

"No, not a cipher Watson. Without seeing it, I believe it is shorthand. Am I correct, Mina?"

"Yes, it is shorthand, Sherlock. Jonathan used that means to keep our messages somewhat out of prying eyes."

"How would you discover that Holmes, without sight of it?" Said I.

"Because, Mina has said that she transcribed it, so it would be installed in such writing that Dracula could not make sense of it, with the solution contained within the capable head of Mrs. Harker. We shall therefore turn to the typewritten version, hoping She formatted it in the way of the written material. So, what of the 1938 Watson?"

"The year then Holmes."

"Hardly, Watson. A year that is yet to be! Not so. Consider the other parts of the cipher. None of them contain a number which could refer to a year, of this or the next century. However, you may yet follow a direction of thought that will prove relevant."

"Let us say that the first two numbers notate a date. Here, Harker's journal arranged by date, such as a book, would be by chapter. Quite appropriate, would not you say? By such reasoning, the first coding date is the 7th of May, or the 5th of July, depending upon the arrangement. Test this conjecture, Watson, move to the dates within the journal."

I flicked through the pages to the first date. The seventh

of May was certainly an entry, somewhat lengthy, taking over nine full pages. The search for the date of the fifth of July took me to the end of the journal.

"Sherlock, upon your reasoning it must be the May seventh to which this theory points, as the journal ends before July."

"Excellent, Watson. Now what of the final number, the 1938."

"Yes, what of it, Sherlock? It cannot be a page number as you point out; the journal does not have so many pages." Said I.

"But it has as many words as contained within it! Nine pages you say. How many words to a line and how many lines to a page?

I counted a sample line and the number of lines on a page.

"Roughly eighteen words to a line and twenty lines to a page." Said I.

"So, for that passage we are looking at over three-thousand words, Watson. Please then count carefully to the 1938th word in the passage from the iteration of May

7."

"Sherlock, the effort of counting to such a number will require some peaceful time. I shall retire to the table to disassemble this cipher. Excuse me, Mrs. Harker, while I do so."

"Be quick to do so Watson, we shall not keep Mina here for longer than this should take."

I thumbed through the pages and found the required passages; I sat in the chair and read the handwritten words. Sherlock remained in his chair and stared into the same flames illuminating the unflinching face of the young woman opposite. Referring to the cipher, I spoke the words as I found them, and it formed thus the passage:

"PURFLEET Carfax Count Dangerous SEWARD Destroy IN England Home NOT Castle Evil WHITBY."

"We have the message!" Said I, "but, what does it mean?"

"Let me see it." Said Mina. "These places and names all relate to Dr. Seward and Carfax, the home of Dracula seven years ago. But he did not destroy Seward. Does he also mean that his home is not his castle? Do you see Mr. Holmes?"

"I think that there is more discovery to be made. We shall put this to one side for the moment. Now, Miss Mina, let us get to the core that you bring before us tonight."

8

AN INSPECTOR CALLS

There was suddenly a loud knocking at the door directly from the street, and after Mrs. Hudson answered it, the sound of furious stamping upon the stairs. Before further discussion could begin and without introduction, Mrs. Hudson flung open the door and, without courtesy or sound, she ushered a man into the room. We all turned towards the lean, rat-faced, sly-looking, dark-eyed fellow who stood before us. Drab clothing, sodden and dripping from its soaking from the elements that ravaged the street, hung from his frame. His shoes squeaking as he made his way closer, standing beside the breakfast table, behind where we sat. The man was Inspector Lestrade, a detective of Scotland Yard. A regular visitor to Baker Street, especially in times of stifled investigation. Mrs. Hudson, nonplussed at the late visitor, returned to her bed with a shrug of good night.

More than once already in his career had Holmes helped Lestrade to attain success, his own sole reward being the intellectual joy of the problem. For this reason, the affection and respect of the inspector for his amateur colleague were profound, and he showed them by the frankness with which he consulted Holmes in every difficulty. Mediocrity knows nothing higher than itself; but talent instantly recognizes genius, and Lestrade had talent enough for his profession to enable him to perceive that there was no humiliation in seeking the help of one who already stood alone in Europe, both in his gifts and in his experience. Holmes was not prone to friendship, but he was tolerant of the inspector, and smiled at the sight of this lean, sly-looking and ferret-like man.

“You are extraordinarily late on today, Mr. Lestrade,” said Holmes. “So, I fear this confirms that there is some mischief afoot.”

"If you said 'hope' instead of 'fear,' it would be nearer the truth, I'm thinking, Mr. Holmes," the inspector answered, with a knowing grin. "I am here, but..."

The inspector had paused and was staring with a look of absolute amazement at the scrap of paper laid flat upon the table now in front of him. It was the sheet upon which I had scrawled the decoded message in large script to make it clearer to read. He leant forward and grabbed it, at the same time slumping into the chair, his arms thumping on the tabletop.

"What is this!" he stammered. "SEWARD! CARFAX! PURFLEET! What is this, Mr. Holmes? Man, it is witchcraft! The devil's work! Where in the name of all that is coincidence did you get those words?"

"Yes, it may very well be the devil's work, but not of coincidence, or of that creature's style, indeed. It is a cipher that Dr. Watson and I have in our hands to solve. But why, what's amiss with the words that you see?"

The inspector looked from one to the other of us in dazed astonishment. "Just this," said he, "not only the words, but their order. A Dr. Seward found murdered this morning! Within the residence of Carfax Estate in Purfleet."

Mina exhaled a gasp. "Oh no, not John!" She rose,

unsteady on her feet, as if suddenly awoken from a dream, looking around as to locate her own whereabouts. She viewed each of us with surprise, the look that is exhibited when you meet a stranger that you have seen somewhere previously.

"Mrs. Harker! What is the matter?" Said I.

"But am I not within a dream of some instant?" She stuttered, placing her hand over her mouth, and sitting with an unsteady recline back into the chair from which she had jumped.

"You do not recall coming into here? To Baker Street?"

"Yes, sir, I remember, but it is as though I entered a realm that was not within my purview to effect. The last I am fully aware of was being at my home in Whitby, with my family. But then I am drawn to London and to your company. I travel here and wake to the reality now, and with this awful news. It cannot be true. Not Dr. Seward!"

"You know of this man?" Asked Lestrade, adding, "I am sorry to be the bearer of such news, I should introduce myself Miss, I am Inspector Lestrade of Scotland Yard. If I may ask you how you know Seward?" Mina looked at the detective, her eyes full of sadness, her complexion whiter than that when she first arrived.

“We were good friends; I have known him for a long time. But how is he dead? What happened to him?”

“We are still investigating the matter, and that is why I am here. I need the help of Sherlock Holmes.”

It was one of those dramatic moments for which my friend existed. It would be an overstatement to say that the amazing announcements shocked him or even excited him. Without having a tinge of cruelty in his singular composition, he was undoubtedly callous from long overstimulation. Yet, if his emotions dulled, his intellectual perceptions became exceedingly active. There was no trace then of the horror which I had myself felt at this curt declaration; but his face showed rather the quiet and interested composure of the chemist who sees the crystals falling into position from his over-saturated solution.

“Remarkable!” said he. “Remarkable!”

“You do not seem surprised.” Said Lestrade.

“Interested, but hardly surprised. Why should it surprise me? I receive an anonymous communication from a quarter which I know to be important, containing a cipher that can now be seen as a warning that danger threatens known persons. That cipher being written at least seven years before it provided us the key to unlock it. That key being delivered by the hand of this young lady, and without doubt outside of her control. Within the hour I learn that this danger has actually materialized, and that a certain person is dead at a precise location, both which are mentioned within the now broken cipher. I am interested; but, as you observe, I am not surprised. We are being led upon an arranged path Mr. Lestrade."

In a few brief sentences, he explained to the inspector the facts about the letter and the cipher. Lestrade sat with his chin on his hands and his sharp features in a puzzled contortion, expressing the incredulousness of the statement. After a moment in thought, he looked directly at Sherlock like a bulldog waiting on a marrow bone.

"I was going down to Purfleet overnight to get there next morning," said he. "I am asking you if you cared to come with me. You and your friend here. But from what you say we might be doing better work in London."

"I rather think not," said Holmes.

“Hang it all, Mr. Holmes!” cried the inspector. “The papers will be full of the Purfleet murder in a day or two; but where’s the mystery if there is a man in London who prophesied the crime before ever it occurred? We have only to lay our hands on that man, and the rest will follow.”

“Inspector, that is of no doubt. But how do you propose to lay evidence upon a man who, when he made this cipher, was seven years away in Transylvania?”

Lestrade turned over the letter which Holmes had handed him. “Posted in Transylvania. 1887.”

“You think there is someone, some force, behind this informant?”

“I know there is.”

“Him. Count Dracula?”

“Exactly! We shall journey to Purfleet with haste.”

9

THE CONFIRMATION

Inspector Lestrade smiled, his narrow lips curling at their points. His left eyelid quivered as he glanced towards me over the table and then to Sherlock as he sat fully reclined in his chair. "I won't conceal from you, Mr. Holmes, that we think in the department that you have a little fixation over this Count. Knowing this, I have, on a previous occasion, made some inquiries myself about this gentleman. He seems to be a very elusive, but also a respectable, learned, and talented sort of man."

"I'm glad you've got so far as to recognize the talent. But a gentleman he is certainly not!"

"Man, you can't but recognize it! I heard your view that he may be a potential suspect when we discussed the attacks on children, as the Gazette reported them some years ago. I made it my business to interview him, as you are in most circumstances, the illuminator of many mysteries. How could I not? I visited him at his estate in Exeter some weeks after the first report. Together we discussed his business in London. He explained his intentions and charitable work. When he put his hand on my shoulder as we were parting, it was like a father's blessing before you go out into the cold, cruel world. The gesture transferred the same great reassurance and comfort that you would receive from his gaze, because his character exuded such."

Holmes chuckled and rubbed his hands together and leant forward in his chair. "Great!" he said. "Great! Tell me, Friend Lestrade, this pleasing and touching interview was, I suppose, in the Count's study, within the south facing part of the building I presume?"

"Well, it was in his study, but I know not of its direction with the compass. Why south, Sherlock?"

"More of that in a moment. A fine room, is it not?" Sherlock pressed his fingertips together and slipped back into a full recline.

"Very fine, very handsome indeed, Mr. Holmes."

"You sat in front of his writing desk with its back to the window?"

"Just so."

"Sun in your eyes, from the south, and his face in the shadow?"

"Well, it was late in the evening, so there was no sun, as it was just going down. But dang it Sherlock, yes, the sunset was behind the fellow! But I mind he turned the lamp on my face to set the brightness from that direction. Just as you do in your own lodgings!"

"It would be. Did you observe any mirrors or reflective materials, such as silver or metal, within the room?"

"I miss little, Mr. Holmes. Maybe I learned that from you. So, no I do not recall any reflective objects in that room. Definitely no mirrors. Dark walls, paneled with portraits of faces unknown to me."

“Did the desk contain fresh fruits of the citrus species, oranges, lemons for example?”

“Why yes, there was a bowl of grapefruit at hand.”

The inspector endeavored to look interested.

“As I expected” Holmes continued, tapping his joined his fingertips together, and pressing further back in his chair until its leather back creaked under his pressure.

The inspector’s eyes grew abstracted. “Hadn’t we better…” he said.

“We are doing so,” Holmes interrupted. “All that I am saying has a very direct and vital bearing upon what you have called the Purfleet Mystery. In fact, it may be called the very center of it.”

Lestrade smiled feebly and looked appealingly to me, his eyelid quivering. “Your thoughts move a bit too quick for me, Mr. Holmes. You leave out a link or two, and I cannot get over the gap. What in the whole wide world can be the connection between the lack of reflective materials, the position of his desk, the orientation of the room, the provision of fresh fruit and the affair at Purfleet?”

“All knowledge comes useful to the detective,” remarked

Holmes.

It was clear that it did. The inspector looked honestly interested within the confines of his puzzlement.

Holmes smiled. Genuine admiration, the characteristic of the proper artist, always warmed him. "What about Purfleet?" he asked.

"We've time yet," said the inspector, glancing at his watch. "I've a cab at the door, and it won't take us twenty minutes to Victoria, where we can ride the night train. But about your expectation and deduction: I thought you told me once, Mr. Holmes, that you had never met Count Dracula, or attended his office or estate?"

"No, I never have."

"Then how do you know about his room?"

"Ah, that's another matter."

"You've got us side-tracked with your interesting anecdotes, Mr. Holmes. What really counts is your remark that there is some connection between the Count and the crime. That you get from the warning received through the man Harker. Can we for our present practical needs get any further than that?"

"We may form some conception as to the motives of the crime. It is, as I gather from your original remarks, an inexplicable, or at least an unexplained, murder. Now, presuming that the source of the crime is as we suspect it to be, there might be two different motives. In the first place, I may tell you that Dracula rules with a rod of iron over his people. His discipline is tremendous. There is only one punishment in his code. It is death, or a kind of death. Now we know that this murdered man, this Seward whose approaching fate known through accidental discovery some years ago by a man who the Count considered being his subordinate, had crossed the Count. His punishment followed and known to all if only to put the fear of death into them."

"Well, that is one suggestion, Mr. Holmes."

"The other is that they have engineered it in the ordinary course of business. Was there any evidence of robbery?"

"I have not heard."

"If so, it would, of course, be against the first hypothesis and in favor of the second. Dracula may have been engaged to engineer it to distract from his chief business. But whichever it may be, or if it is some third combination, it is down at Purfleet and the Carfax estate that we must seek the solution. I know our man too well to suppose that he has left anything up here which may lead us to him."

"Then to Purfleet we must go!" cried Lestrade, jumping from his chair. "My word! It is later than I thought. I can give you, gentlemen, five minutes for preparation, and that is all."

"And ample for us both," said Holmes, as he sprang up and hastened to change from his dressing gown to his coat. "While we are on our way, inspector, we will listen to Mrs. Harker, who I invite to ride with us. Mina will relay the story of the last known sighting of Dracula at his homestead in Transylvania. If you would be good enough to travel with us and tell us all about it, Mrs. Harker?"

10

DIRT AND DUST

Together, our four, Sherlock, Mina, Lestrade and I, strode directly to the horse-drawn cab waiting in front of 221B Baker Street. The weather still as blustery and cold as we had imagined from the warm confines of the apartment and the blazing fire, if not more so. The effect of the persistent deluge upon the poor bedraggled horse, complete with oilskin jacket wrapped around its flanks, being particularly unkind, fidgeting back and forth, its feet dancing on the rain-soaked cobbles. We shook off the elements of the night before stepping up into the coach and closing the door tightly behind us. Inside there was a sort of respite and a moment of silence as we gathered our individual thoughts.

Sherlock sat beside me, with Mina directly opposite. A deliberate maneuver. He meant to observe both her and Lestrade's expressions as Mina unfolded the story of Dracula's last moments, as she had seen them.

"Now, we have a brief ride to Victoria, some thirty minutes depending upon the humor of the horse at hand, with further dependency on whether the route is nearer supper and a dry stable, no doubt. Mina, please if you would favor us with the facts of the last meeting with the Count. Only as you recall it. That is important."

"Why yes, of course Sherlock, although my thoughts and recollections may not be entirely clear as I have been greatly affected by the horrific news of Dr. Seward."

"Yes, an awful thing it is." I said, consoling Mrs. Harker as her eyes again formed glassy pockets of tears in each.

"Mrs. Harker, you must try to put that to one side for the moment. We only have a small amount of time before we reach our train. We will deposit you at a hotel near Victoria so that you may rest, before travelling home." Said Sherlock, displaying his impatience and lack of any empathy that may be due in such circumstance. However, as in most circumstances that he engaged, his calculation worked; Mrs. Harker spurred into animated explanation, her voice bursting with information like a rapid-fire gun.

Sherlock Holmes's eyes glistened, not through sadness, but through interest. His pale cheeks took a warmer hue, and his whole eager face shone with an inward light as the story revealed itself. Leaning forward in the cab, he listened intently to Mina's sketch of the encounter, nodding as she spoke and pressing his fingertips together as his arms rested upon his thighs.

"We were to ambush the Count as he travelled back to his home. Professor Van Helsing, and I settled into a natural hollow in a rock on the side of a mountain close to Dracula's castle. The light was dimming as the day was ending in flurries of snow. The winter was upon us. Van Helsing stood on top of a nearby mound and using his field-glasses suddenly called out:"

"Look! Madam Mina, look! Look! I sprang up and stood beside him on the mound; he handed me his glasses and pointed. The snow was now falling more heavily, and swirled about fiercely, for a high wind was blowing, whistling through the branches of the forest. When there were pauses between the snow flurries, I could see a long way into the distance. From the height where we were it was possible to see far off, beyond the white waste of snow that was deepened by the minute. I could see the river, lying like a black coiled snake in kinks and curls as it wound its way in the valley. Straight in front of us and not far off, in fact, so near that I wondered we had not noticed before, came a group of mounted men hurrying along. Amid them was a cart, a long flat-bed wagon which swept from side to side, like a dog's tail wagging, with each bump and ditch within the road. Outlined against the snow as they were, I could see from the men's clothes that they were peasants or gypsies."

"This Van Helsing, he is an expert in such matters?" Asked Sherlock.

"Yes, he is the one person who can fathom the behavior of this monster. He has the tools and knowledge to dispatch him."

"Where is Van Helsing at this moment?"

"He is in Amsterdam, the last that I am aware."

"Thank you, please continue."

"We saw the caravan approaching. On the cart was a great square wooden chest. My heart leapt as I saw it, for I felt the end was coming. For a moment a dizziness beset me. My mind seemed to be overtaken by the thought of evil, and I stumbled on my feet. The evening was now drawing close, and well I knew that at sunset the thing, which was till then imprisoned in the box, would take new freedom and could in any of many forms elude all pursuit. In fear I turned to the Professor; to my consternation, however, he was not there. An instant later, I saw him below me. Around the mound he had taken a stick and drawn a circle. When he had completed it, he stood beside me again, saying, 'At least you shall be safe here from him!' He took the glasses from me, and at the next lull of the snow swept the entire space below us. See, he said, 'they come quickly; they are flogging the horses and galloping as hard as they can.' He paused and went on in a hollow voice. 'They are racing for the sunset. We may be too late. God's will be done!' Down came another blinding rush of driving snow, and it blotted the entire landscape out. It soon passed, however, and once more something fixed his glasses on the plain. Then came a sudden cry:"

"Look! Look! Look! See, two horsemen follow fast, coming up from the south. It must be Quincey and John. Take the glass. Look before the snow blots it all out! I took it and looked. The two men might be Dr. Seward and Mr. Morris. I knew at all events that neither of them was Jonathan. I knew Jonathan was not far off; looking around, I noticed on the north side of the joining party two other men, riding at full speed. Their horses pulling up the snow behind them as they galloped towards the party with the cart. One of them I knew was Jonathan, and the other I took, of course, to be Lord Godalming. When I told the Professor, he hollered in glee like he was a young boy again, and, after looking intently till a snow fall made sight hopeless, he laid his Winchester rifle ready for use against a boulder at the opening of our shelter. 'They are all converging,' he said. 'When the time comes, we shall have gypsies on all sides.' I got out my revolver ready to hand, for whilst we were speaking the howling of wolves came louder and closer. When the snowstorm abated for a moment, we looked again. It was strange to see the snow falling in such heavy flakes close to us, and beyond, the sun shining more and more brilliantly as it sank down towards the far mountain tops. Sweeping the glass all around us I could see here and there dots moving singly and in twos and threes and greater numbers, the wolves were assembling for their prey."

"Every instant seemed an age whilst we waited. The wind

came now in fierce bursts, and it drove the snow with fury as it swept upon us in circling eddies. At its worst, we could not see an arm's length before us; but at others, as the hollow-sounding wind swept by us, it seemed to clear the airspace around us so that we could see far off. We had of late been so accustomed to watch for sunrise and sunset, that we knew with fair accuracy when it would be; and we knew that before long the sun would set. I could not believe that by our watches it was less than an hour that we waited in that rocky shelter before the various bodies converged close upon us. The wind came now with fiercer and more bitter sweeps, and more steadily from the north. It had driven the snow clouds from us, for, with only occasional bursts, the snow fell."

"We could clearly differentiate the individuals of each party, the pursued and the pursuers. Strangely enough, those pursued did not seem to recognize, or at least to care, that we pursued them; they seemed, however, to quicken with heightened speed as the sun dipped lower and lower on the mountain tops."

"Closer and closer they drew. The Professor and I crouched down behind our rock and held our weapons ready; I could see that he determined they should not pass. One and all were unaware of our presence."

"All at once two voices shouted out to: 'Halt!' One was my Jonathan's, raised in a high key of passion, the other Mr. Morris' strong, resolute tone of quiet command. The gypsies may not have known the language, but there was no mistaking the tone, in whatever tongue the words spoken. An order to defend and protect. Instinctively they reined in, and at the instant Lord Godalming and Jonathan dashed up at one side and Dr. Seward and Mr. Morris on the other. The leader of the gypsies, a massive muscular fellow who sat on his horse like a centaur, waved them back, and in a fierce voice gave to his companions some word to proceed. They lashed the horses which sprang forward; but the four men raised their Winchester rifles, and unmistakably commanded them to stop. At the same moment, Professor Van Helsing and I climbed behind the rock and positioned our weapons at them. Surrounded, the men tightened their reins and drew up. The leader gestured to them and gave a word at which every man of the gypsy party drew what weapon he carried, knife or pistol, and held himself in readiness to attack. They joined the fight in an instant."

"The leader, with a quick movement of his rein, threw his horse out in front, and pointing first to the sun, now close on the hilltops, and then to the castle, said something which I did not understand. For answer, all four men of our party threw themselves from their horses and dashed towards the cart. I should have felt terrible fear at seeing Jonathan in such danger, but that the ardor of battle must have been upon me as well as the rest of them; I felt no fear, but only a wild, surging desire to do something. Seeing the quick movement of our parties, the leader of the gypsies made a command; his men instantly formed round the cart in a sort of undisciplined endeavor, each one shouldering and shoving the other in his fervor to carry out the order."

"During this I could see that Jonathan on one side of the ring of men, and Quincey on the other, were forcing a way to the cart; they were bent on finishing their task before the sun should set. Nothing seemed to stop or even to hinder them. Neither the levelled weapons nor the flashing knives of the gypsies in front, nor the howling of the wolves behind, appeared to even engage their attention. Jonathan's impetuosity, and the manifest singleness of his purpose, seemed to overwhelm those in front of him; instinctively they recoiled, aside and let him pass."

"In an instant he had jumped upon the cart, and, with a strength which seemed incredible, raised the great box, and flung it over the wheel to the ground. In the meantime, Mr. Morris had reason to apply much force to pass through his side of the ring of men. All the time I had been breathlessly watching Jonathan. I had, with the tail of my eye, seen him pressing desperately forward, and had seen the knives of the gypsies' flash as he won a way through them, and they cut at him."

"He had parried with his great bowie knife, and at first, I thought that he too had come through in safety; but as he sprang beside Jonathan, who had by now jumped from the cart, I could see that with his left hand he was clutching at his side, and that the blood was spurting through his fingers. He did not delay notwithstanding this, for as Jonathan, with desperate energy, attacked one end of the chest, attempting to prize off the lid with his great kukri knife, he attacked the other frantically with his Bowie. Under the efforts of both men, the lid yielded; the nails drew with a quick screeching sound, and it threw the top of the box back and away from the cart."

"By this time the gypsies, seeing themselves covered by the Winchesters, and at the mercy of Lord Godalming and Dr. Seward, had given in and made no resistance. The sun was almost down on the mountain tops, and the shadows of the entire group fell long upon the snow. I saw the

Count lying within the box upon the earth, some of which the jolt of falling from the cart had scattered over him. He was deathly pale, just like a waxen image, and the red eyes glared with the horrible vindictive look which I knew too well."

"As I looked, the eyes saw the sinking sun, and the look of hate in them turned to triumph. But, on the instant, came the sweep and flash of Jonathan's great knife. I shrieked as I saw it shear through the throat; whilst at the same moment Mr. Morris's bowie knife plunged into the heart."

"It was like a miracle; but before our very eyes, and almost in the drawing of a breath, the whole-body crumble into dust and passed from our sight."

"The end Mrs. Harker?" Said Sherlock.

"We watched as Quincey took his last breath, his side pierced fully with a blade of the gypsies. The ground soaked with the brave man's blood. We loaded his body onto the wagon from which the box had fallen and set out to return to the town."

"What about the box?"

"Why it was now only a box of dirt and dust Mr. Holmes. We left it where it had fallen. Open, its contents spilled and exposed to the freezing weather."

"Only dirt and dust, Mina? There is more to be discovered here, and I'll wager that you already know that!"

11

THE CARFAX ESTATE

“Dirt and dust” proved to be disappointingly little to go on, I determined, but yet there was sufficient to persuade us that the case before us might well be worthy of the expert’s closest attention. Sherlock brightened and rubbed his thin hands together as he refined the meagre but remarkable details. A long series of sterile weeks lay behind us, and here at last there was a fitting object for those remarkable talents which, like all special gifts, become irksome to their owner when they are not in use. That razor brain blunted and rusted with inaction. He enthused, and it was gratifying to see the mind of such a man brightening at the challenge.

We arrived at Victoria and said our goodbyes to Mrs. Harker. She informed us she would return to her home in Whitby sometime the next day. Sherlock promised he would be in touch by telegram and to my surprise showed that he may need to visit her within the next week.

On the train to Purfleet, the Inspector was himself dependent, as he explained to us, upon a scribbled account forwarded to him before he arrived at Baker Street. Lewis Shore, the local officer, was a personal acquaintance, and hence Lestrade had been notified much more promptly than is usual at Scotland Yard when provincials need their help. It is a cold scent upon which they typically asked the Metropolitan expert to run.

“DEAR INSPECTOR LESTRADE (said the message which he read to us):”

“The official requisition for your services is by separate delivery. This is for your private eye. Telegraph me what train you can get for Purfleet, and I will meet it, or have it met if I am too occupied. This case is a conundrum and exquisite, things do not add up. We shall not waste a moment in getting started. If you can bring Mr. Holmes, please do so; for he will find something after his own heart. We would think they had fixed the whole up for theatrical effect if there was not a dead man in the middle of it. My word! It IS a snorter."

"Your friend seems to be no fool," remarked Holmes.

"No, sir, Lewis Shore is a remarkably live man, if I am any authority."

"Well, have you anything more?"

"Only that he will give us every detail when we meet."

"Then how did you get to the conclusion that it was Dr. Seward and the fact that he has been horribly murdered?"

"That information was in the enclosed official report. Although it did not say 'horrible': that is not a recognized official term. It gave the name Dr. Seward. The document disclosed his injuries had been in the throat. It also mentioned the hour of the alarm, which was close on to midday today, many hours it seems after the crime had occurred. The body being cold and with a rigor set within. The report added that the case was undoubtedly one of murder, but that no arrest was made, and that the case was one which presented some very perplexing and extraordinary features. There were no immediate suspects. That is doubtless all we have at present, Mr. Holmes."

"Then, with your permission, we will leave it at that, inspector. The temptation to form premature theories upon insufficient data is the bane of our profession. I can see only two things for certain at present; an informer, of seven years past who was at the time the note issued, imprisoned in Transylvania and a dead man in Purfleet. It is the chain between that we are going to trace."

Now for a moment I will ask leave to remove my own insignificant personality and to describe events which occurred before we arrived upon the scene by the light of knowledge which came to us afterwards. Only in this way can I make the reader appreciate the people concerned and the remarkable setting in which their fate was cast.

Prior to our exit from Baker Street, I had pulled a copy of the History of Essex by W. White from the bookshelf. I opened to the page that described the place of Purfleet. The tiny village had to it only five hundred inhabitants. There was also a barracks that housed two hundred soldiers. Purfleet is a village and military station, at the mouth of a rivulet, and at the west end of West Thurrock. Near it are the extensive chalk pits. The harbor is often full of shipping business and animation: and joining it is a large government powder magazine, comprising five detached bomb-proof and well-protected storehouses, barracks for a company of artillery, a storekeeper's mansion, and a good quay. The magazine has room for the safe keeping of sixty thousand barrels of gunpowder. Enough to blow the entire town into the river.

The lord would live in the ancient manor house known as the Carfax, about half a mile from the town, standing in an old park famous for its enormous beech trees. There are but few houses close at hand, one being a sizeable house only recently added to and formed into a private lunatic asylum which itself houses over twenty inmates. It is not, however, visible from the grounds.

The Carfax Estate holds an intriguing history to it as I investigated its character further. Part of this venerable building dates back to the time of the first crusade, when Hugo de Capus built a fortalice in the center of the estate, granted to him by the Red King. The original building being consumed by fire in 1543. A new country house rose upon the ruins of the feudal castle. Some of the smoke-blackened corner stones used in the re-building. The name of the estate is no doubt a corruption of the old

Quatre Face, as the house is four-sided, agreeing with the cardinal points of the compass. The house itself is still much as the builder had left it in the early seventeenth century.

The estate contains in all some twenty acres, surrounded by a solid stone wall. There are many trees on it, which make it in places gloomy, and there is a broad, dark-looking pond or small lake, evidently fed by some springs, as the water is clear and flows away in a fair-sized stream. Of the double moats which had guarded its more warlike ancestor, the outer had progressively dried up through lack of upkeep. And served the humble function of a kitchen garden.

The inner one was still there, and lay forty feet in breadth, though now only a few feet in depth. It circled around the complete house. A small stream fed it and continued beyond it, so that the sheet of water, though turbid, was never ditch like or unhealthy. The house is enormous and imagines all periods previous, back to medieval times. Only a few windows broke the brick elevation. All high up, some heavily barred with iron.

The only access to the house is over a drawbridge, the

chains and windlass of which for a while been inoperable by their rust. The latest tenants of the Manor House had, however, with characteristic energy, set this right, and the drawbridge was not only capable of being raised, but actually raised every evening and lowered every morning. By thus renewing the custom of the old feudal days, the action converted the Manor House into an island during the night. A fact which had a very direct bearing upon the mystery which was soon to engage the attention of all England.

.

12

THE RESURRECTION

Now I know the sequence of events that led to this point. The reader should be mindful that I developed this event from a detailed analysis of facts which are yet to be found. The purpose of this chapter is so I may record the story in its progression. And to introduce the antagonist of this happening. This track had begun, we know, seven years since Mina, Jonathan, Professor Van Helsing, Godalming, and Dr. Seward had returned to English shores, imbued with the victory that they had won with their own hands, but with the misery of losing their comrade and good friend, Quincey Morris. Slain in the battle to extinguish the Count. They left a harsh winter behind them. It was then 1887.

The spring following their return came to the Carpathian Mountains and ultimately to the resting place of Dracula's dust, mixed with the dirt from the box that once carried it. The material spilled upon the ground and frozen in place as a heap of dirt. It had maintained its innate vitality throughout the dark and cold winter.

Overlooking the scene, the castle remained empty, casting a gruesome shadow over the valley. The winter brought with it a peacefulness to the area. The gypsies had moved on to warmer pastures and the wolves quietened. Released from their fears and superstitions, the local population was going more about their business than previous circumstances had allowed them. They celebrated the New Year with all the vigor that the villagers could muster. For once, families looked to the coming of Spring and the warmer air. And to freedom from evil.

Early April saw the hastening of the thaw. The winter had been a harsh one, and the snow had reached a considerable depth and would take some time to melt back. Great blocks of the frozen white blanket still caught in time, draped upon the branches of the evergreen trees of the forest. The weight bending the limbs of the trees like the arch of a bow. Small streams and springs around the mountain, bubbling with fresh water, provided evidence that the melt was underway further up the slope. Day by day, the gentle heat from the sun's light as it barely made it through the fingers of the forest warmed the canopies and, where it passed, the hard tundra frozen beneath.

Snow, now caught in the light, lost its grip, falling, following random drips of clear water, which provided a steady aim to the ground. The branches springing back into place once disturbed to release their cargo.

The rocks and soil in under the steps of the last battle emerged from their shroud of snow. From underneath this blanket, the last resting place of Quincey Morris revealed itself. The spot clearly marked by the substantial loss of blood he suffered because of his fatal wound. A dark crimson stain of the corpuscles frozen into the shape of a single butterfly wing. The life which the fluid had once supported held in place by the cold and darkness, a perfect preservative. Until now.

As the snow melted, the clear ice-cold water it produced flowed down the gradient and over the rocky ground towards the frozen blood-stained reservoir. The tentacles ran with gravity, washing and pulling from the ground the frozen lifeblood from its store. Carrying it further, the water now a pink hue, flowing by gravity towards the upturned box and mixture of dirt and dormant dust. A mix containing the remains of Dracula, still undead. With no time, a translucent vapor emitted itself from the pile of dirt as they combined the nutrients of the blood, feeding whatever remained within the dust.

The dirt bubbled and foamed like a boiling kettle; a vapor rose. The outer edges of the swirling gas solidified. A shape emerged, an opaque darkness that increased in density from the outer to the inner. The revitalized corpuscles drawn upwards, forming channels of red liquid, capillaries filling, bones straightening, organs manufacturing, muscles tightening, and skin stretching. Groaning, bending, until a figure of a living thing, yet a man, clawing its reformed limbs skyward. Issuing from its new throat a bone curdling howl as the ultimate embodiment animated into view.

The howl drew a chilling reply from the forest. From all directions. Wolves calling back without delay, getting closer and louder. Opening slowly, the eyes of the figure focused and raised themselves. Now positively blazing with the fire within, a hate held at bay then released. The red light lurid, as if the flames of hellfire blazed behind them. Appearing through the organization of cells, the face, a deathly pale, the lines of it were heavy like drawn wires; the thick eyebrows sprouted and met over the nose, now seemed like a heaving bar of white-hot molten alloy. With a fierce sweep of an arm, the form hurled its hand towards the silhouette of the castle high on the ridge above and pointed. Then the figure motioned to the wolves as they gathered around in a circle. In an imperious gesture and in a voice which, though low and almost a whisper, seemed to cut through the air, said.

"They know not who they deal with, and of the power and evil that lies at my disposal. I Dracula, creator, and master of the undead hold all within my hand. At once we shall return to the castle that stands above this region and the world. Now, my friends, go before me and remove the impediments laid at the entrances to the building, the pungent plant, and those holy wafers. The six will all pay dearly for their plan and will regret taking motion against me, the fools!"

On this command the wolves ran as a pack toward the

castle, Dracula shifted his shape into the familiar form of the lizard that Jonathan had observed during his imprisonment, and darted into the shadows, scurrying on his belly, to avoid the polka dot pattern of sunlight that had evaded the canopy above. The wolves scratched and dug at the still frozen ground around the castle. Providing enough break in the building's defense to facilitate entry. Dracula arrived soon afterwards, still as a crawling beast; its fingers tipped with pointed claws.

In one movement the creature leapt onto the stone wall, still in shadow, and ascended with tremendous speed to the window of his quarters. The defense breached; he was home, and would sleep today and then, over the next six years, plan his return to England to issue horrific vengeance over the ones who had wronged him. That plan now instigated. He had already set parts of it to motion.

13

THE PURFLEET MYSTERY

All the following details I noted afterwards, after interviewing those involved and deducting, with the help of Mr. Holmes, the nature of the mystery. It was at nine forty-five in the morning that the first alarm reached the small local police station. The office was in the charge of Sergeant Wilson of the Essex Constabulary. Waverly, an orderly employed at the asylum in the grounds of the estate, in much excitement, had rushed up to the door of the station and hammered furiously upon its knocker. Out of breath, it took him some minutes to relay his message. A terrible tragedy had occurred at the Manor House. Dr. Seward was inside and having been found dead in the apartment he used for his work with the asylum adjacent. Waverly had hurried back to the house, followed within a few minutes by the police sergeant, who arrived at the scene a little after ten o'clock, after taking prompt steps to warn the county authorities that something serious was afoot.

On reaching the Manor House, the sergeant had found the drawbridge lowered, and the windows covered with curtains to preserve the darkness inside. Waverly opened the door which was nearest to the entrance, and he had beckoned to the sergeant to follow him. At that moment there arrived Dr. Wood, a brisk and capable general practitioner from the village. The three men entered the fatal apartment and its bedroom together, while the horror-stricken housekeeper followed at their heels, closing the door behind them to shut out the terrible scene from others circulating in the building.

Dr. Seward lay on his back, sprawled with outstretched limbs in the center of the room. He was clad only in a white dressing gown, which covered his night clothes. There were carpet slippers on his bare feet. The doctor knelt beside him and held down the hand lamp which had stood on the table. One glance at the victim was enough to show the healer that his presence could be dispensed with. The face of the body was pale, an anemic pallor to the flesh. There was no sign of life.

The doctor had taken the lamp and was narrowly scrutinizing the body. "What's this mark?" he asked. "Could this have any connection with the crime?"

The dead man's neck held two small red puncture holes, standing out in vivid relief upon the lard-colored skin.

"I do not profess to know the meaning of it," said Cecil Waverly; "but I have seen the mark on Dr. Seward many times these last few weeks."

"This case will make a stir, sir," Wilson remarked. "It beats anything I have seen, and I am no chicken."

"You can take him to the mortuary now," he said. "There is nothing more to be learned." Said Dr. Wood.

The country police officer was unnerved and troubled by the tremendous responsibility which had come so suddenly upon him. "We will touch nothing until my superiors arrive," he said in a hushed voice, staring in horror at the dreadful face of Seward.

“Nothing has been touched up to now,” said Waverly. “I’ll answer for that. You see it all exactly as I found it.”

“When was that?” The sergeant had drawn out his notebook.

“It was just half-past eight this morning. I had dressed, and on my way from my quarters on the lower floor to meet with Dr. Seward before our rounds at the asylum, which we normally begun at nine.”

“Was the door open?”

“No, it was closed. I knocked and received no answer, so I entered, calling his name. But then I noticed that poor Dr. Seward was lying, as you see him. His bedroom candle was still burning on the table. It was I who lit the lamp some minutes afterward. The curtains were still drawn closed.”

“Did you see no one?”

“No, not a soul.”

“No. then I heard Mrs. Douglas, the housekeeper, coming up the stair behind me, and I rushed out to prevent her from seeing this dreadful sight.”

"But surely I have heard that they keep the drawbridge up all night."

"Yes, it was until I lowered it before making my way to Dr. Seward's room."

"Then how could any murderer have got away? It is out of the question!"

"At what o'clock was it raised?"

"It was nearly six o'clock," said Waverley.

"I've heard," said the sergeant, "that it was usually raised at sunset. That would be nearer half-past four than six at this time of year."

Then the sergeant noticed and then picked up a note which lay close to the body and a lone candlestick.

"What's this?" he asked, holding the small scrap of paper at eye level between his finger and thumb.

Waverly looked at it with curiosity. "I never noticed it before," he said. "The murderer must have left it behind him. Some sort of message it seems."

The worthy country police officer shook his head. "Seems to me the sooner we get London on to this case, the better," said he. "Lewis Shore is a smart man. No local job has ever been too much for Lewis Shore. It will be some time later today before he is here to help us. But I expect we will have to look to London before we are through. Anyhow, I'm not ashamed to say that it is a deal too thick for the likes of me."

14

THE BURNT CRUCIFIX

At eleven o'clock this morning the senior Essex detective, Lewis Shore, a quiet, comfortable-looking person in a loose tweed suit, with a clean-shaved, ruddy face, a stout body and close-cropped blond hair. Resembling more of a small farmer, a retired gamekeeper, or anything upon earth except a very favorable specimen of the provincial criminal officer. Responded to the urgent call from Sergeant Wilson, arrived at Carfax from headquarters in a carriage behind a breathless horse, to examine the scene.

By the one-thirty train he had sent his message to Scotland Yard, and was at the Purfleet station at eleven-thirty that night to welcome the three of us.

"A real downright snorter, Mr. Lestrade!" he kept repeating. "We'll have the pressmen down like flies when they understand it. I am hoping we will get our work done before they get poking their noses into it and messing up all the trails. There has been nothing like this that I can remember. There are some bits that will come home to you, Mr. Holmes, or I am mistaken. And you also, Dr. Watson; for the physicians will have a word to say before we conclude.

In ten minutes, we settled in the cab of his carriage and were being served a swift sketch of those events outlined in the previous chapter. Lestrade made an occasional note; while Holmes sat absorbed, with the expression of surprised and reverent admiration with which the botanist studies the unique and precious bloom.

"Remarkable!" he said, when the story was unfolded, "most remarkable! I can hardly recall any case where the features have been more peculiar."

"I thought you would say so, Mr. Holmes," said Shore in great delight. "We're well up with the times in Essex. I have told you how matters were, up to the time when I took over from Sergeant Wilson earlier this evening. My word! I made the old mare go! But I need not have been in such a hurry; for there was nothing immediate that I could do. Sergeant Wilson had all the facts. I checked them and considered them and maybe noticed a few of my own."

As we entered the Carfax Estate and the Manor House, Sergeant Wilson was standing by the doorway to the scene, and greeted my companion, Lestrade and myself. Immediately my attention focused upon the single grim, motionless figure which lay stretched upon the carpeted boards. Open, vacant, sightless eyes staring up at the discolored ceiling.

It was that of a man about thirty years of age, middle-sized, broad shouldered, with crisp curling black hair, and a short stubbly beard. His hands clenched into fists, and his arms thrown abroad, while his lower limbs interlocked as though his death struggle had been a grievous one. On his unyielding face there stood an expression of horror, and as it seemed to me, of hatred, such as I have never seen upon human features.

This malignant and terrible contortion gave the dead man the appearance of a slaughtered farm beast, which was increased by his writhing, unnatural posture. I have seen death in many forms, but never has it appeared to me in a more fearsome aspect than in that dark room.

"Dr. Seward must have pierced his own neck and bled to death." Said Wilson.

"Although there is not enough blood in this room to fill a teacup." Said Sherlock.

Then Waverly drew aside the curtain, and showed that the long, diamond-paned window was open to a minimal gap. "And look at this!" He held the lamp down and illuminated a smudge of blood like the mark of a footprint on the wooden sill. "Someone has stood there in getting out. Someone with naked feet moreover."

"You mean that someone climbed down the wall and stepped across the moat, in bare feet?" Said Lestrade.

"Exactly!"

"And tell me, but how did the perpetrator lower themselves to the ground?"

"The distance to the ground is too great a leap, and there

are not enough footholds in the stone for anyone to climb upon the wall. We did not find a rope or ladder, so they must have taken it with them as they left. I have not a doubt about it. I wish to heaven that I had gone towards the window! But the curtain screened it, as you can see, and so it never occurred to me. Then I heard the step of Mrs. Douglas, and I could not let her enter the room. It would have been too horrible."

"Horrible enough!" said Holmes, looking at the distorted face and the minimal splattering of blood which surrounded it. "I've never seen such injuries to the neck cause death without sufficient evidence of blood. It seems incredible that the body contains almost none. With such a struggle and expression of death that describes a fight against immense suffering. Yet there are no other marks!"

"But, I say," remarked the police sergeant, whose slow, bucolic common sense was still pondering the open window. "It's all very well you saying that a man escaped by wading this moat, but what I ask you is, how did he ever get into the house at all if the bridge was up?"

"Ah, that's the question," said Holmes.

Sherlock approached the body and, kneeling down,

examined it intently. “You are sure that there is no other wound than the punctures upon the neck?” he asked, noting that there were only small splashes of blood which lay close to the body. Nowhere else.

“Positive!”

Sherlock’s nimble fingers were flying here, there, and everywhere, feeling, pressing, unbuttoning, examining, while his eyes wore the same far-away expression which I have already remarked upon. So swiftly was the examination made that one would hardly have guessed the minuteness with which it was conducted. Finally, he sniffed the dead man’s clothing, and then glanced at the collar of the man’s shirt.

“They have not moved him at all?” he asked.

“Only as was necessary for our examination.”

“Let me see the note.” Said I.

“Sherlock, it bears the same cipher that we have just broken from the journal! We will need the transcription to decode this sequence, ‘5-5-62, 5-5-57, OR, 28-5-644, 25-6-269, D’. But how did the cipher appear on this note in the first instance? It cannot be from the same author, can it?”

"How so indeed, Watson. We will first find the solution to the code before attaching an author to it. You may also recall the description of the appearance of such marks on the neck in more than one journal in our hands at Baker Street."

"Yes, but I am inclined to think that it is 'him', the creature not yet destroyed!" I whispered.

Waverly had a makeshift stretcher and four men at hand. At his call they entered the room, and Dr. Seward lifted on to it and carried out. As they raised him, the whole thing wobbled and a distorted and burned crucifix tinkled down from his sleeve and tumbled across the floor. Lestrade grabbed it up and stared at it with mystified eyes.

15

THE WINDOW MYSTERY

After a night's rest and a hearty breakfast, Tuesday morning at the local hotel brought us to further investigation. We set out on foot together towards the estate. We walked down the quaint village street with a row of well-trimmed elms creating a clear edge to the path. Just beyond were two ancient stone pillars, weather-stained and lichen-blotched, bearing upon their summits a shapeless something which had once been the rampant lion of Capus of Purfleet.

A short walk along the winding drive with such sward

and oaks around it as one only sees in rural England. Then a sudden turn, and the long, low Jacobean house of dingy, liver-colored brick lay before us, with an old-fashioned garden of cut yews on each side. As we approached it, there was the wooden drawbridge and the beautiful broad moat, as still and luminous as a mirror in the cold, early winter sunshine.

Three centuries had flowed past the old Manor House. Centuries of births and of homecomings, of country dances and of the meetings of fox hunters. Strange that now in its old age this dark business should have cast its shadow upon the venerable walls! And yet those strange, peaked roofs and quaint, overhung gables were a fitting covering to grim intrigue. As I looked at the deep-set windows and the long sweep of the dull-colored, water-lapped front, I felt that no more fitting scene could be set for such a tragedy.

“That’s the window,” said Detective Shore. “That one on the immediate right of the drawbridge. It’s open just as we found it last night.”

“It looks rather narrow for a man to pass.”

“Well, it wasn’t a large man, anyhow. We do not need

your deductions, Mr. Holmes, to tell us that. But you or I could squeeze through all right."

Holmes walked to the edge of the moat and looked across. Then he examined the stone ledge and the grass border beyond it.

"I've had a good look, Mr. Holmes," said Shore. "There is nothing there, no sign that anyone has landed, or marks of the standing of a ladder, but why should he leave any sign?"

"Exactly. Why should he? Is the water always turbid?"

"Generally, it is about this color. The stream brings down the brown clay."

"How deep is it?"

"About two feet at each side and three in the middle."

"So, we can put aside all idea of the man having drowned in crossing."

Lestrade shook his obstinate head. "I'm not convinced yet that there was ever anyone that should not be in the house." Said he. "I am asking you to consider. I am asking you to consider what it involves if you suppose this murderer came into the house through that window. Oh, my, it is just inconceivable! It is clean against common sense! I put it to you, Mr. Holmes, judging it by what we have heard."

"Well, state your case, Lestrade," said Holmes in his most judicial style.

"The person is not a burglar, supposing that he ever existed. The crucifix business and the card point to premeditated murder for some private reason. Here is a man who slips into a house with the deliberate intention of committing murder. He knows, if he knows anything, that he will have a difficulty in making his escape, as the house is surrounded with water. Then he could hope when the deed was done to slip quickly from the window, by rope or ladder, to wade through the moat, and to get away at his leisure. That is understandable. But is it understandable that he should bring with him a container to take away the blood, is that credible, Mr. Holmes?"

"Well, you put the case strongly," my friend replied thoughtfully. "It certainly needs a good deal of justification. May I ask, Mr. Lewis Shore, whether you examined the farther side of the moat at once to see if there were any signs of the man having climbed out from the water?"

"There were no signs, Mr. Holmes."

"No tracks or marks?"

"None."

"I have worked with Mr. Holmes before," said Inspector Lestrade. "He plays the game."

"My idea of the game, at any rate," said Holmes, with a smile. "I go into a case to help the ends of justice and the work of the police. If I have ever separated myself from the official force, it is because they have first separated themselves from me. I have no wish ever to score at their expense. Mr. Lewis Shore, I claim the right to work in my own way and give my results at my own time, complete rather than in stages."

"I am sure your presence honors us, and we will intend to show you all we know," said Shore cordially. "Come along, Dr. Watson, and when the time comes, we'll all hope for a place in your book."

We walked across the drawbridge, and found admission through a quaint, gnarled, dried-up person, who was the groundskeeper, Ames. The poor old fellow was white and quivering from the shock. The village sergeant, a tall, formal, melancholy man, still held his vigil in the room of fate.

"Anything fresh, Sergeant Wilson?" asked Lewis Shore.

"No, sir."

"Then you can go home. You have had enough. We can send for you if we want you. The groundskeeper had better wait outside. Tell him to warn Mr. Waverly and Mrs. Douglas, that we may want a word with them presently. Now, gentlemen, perhaps you will allow me to give you the views I have formed first, and then you will arrive at your own."

He impressed me, this country specialist. He had a solid grip of fact and a cool, clear, common-sense brain, which should take him some way in his profession. Holmes listened to him intently, with no sign of that impatience which the official exponent too often produced.

"Is it suicide, or is it murder, that's our first question, gentlemen, is it not? If it were suicide, then we are made to believe that this man began by piercing his own throat; that he then opened the window concealed behind the curtain in order to give the idea someone had waited for him, opened the window, put blood on the sill using his own naked foot." Said Shore.

"We can surely dismiss that," said Lestrade.

"So, I think. Suicide is out of the question. Then a murder committed. What we have to determine is, whether someone outside or inside the house did it." Shore Continued.

"Well, let us hear the argument." Said Holmes.

"There are considerable difficulties both ways, and yet one or the other it must be. We will suppose first that some person or persons inside the house did the crime. They got this man when everything was still. They then did the deed and drained the body of its lifeblood. That does not seem a likely start, does it?"

"No, it does not."

"Well, everyone is agreed. It is impossible!"

"You put it clearly," said Holmes. "I am inclined to side with you." he continued:

"Gentlemen, we are driven back to the theory that someone from outside did it. We are still faced with some big difficulties; but anyhow they have ceased to be impossibilities. The murderer got into this room after dusk and after the time when the bridge was raised." Sherlock turned his attention to the groundskeeper.

"Now, Ames, did you observe any marks on Dr. Seward in the past few days?"

"Yes, sir, he said he had cut himself in shaving yesterday morning and had placed a sticking bandage upon it."

"Where on his face Ames?"

"Why, on his neck, right here it was." Ames pointed to the right-side of his neck at the region of the jugular.

"Did you ever know him to cut himself in shaving before?"

"Not for a very long time, sir. He had a steady hand for such matters."

"Had you noticed anything unusual in his conduct, yesterday, Ames?"

"I realized he was a little restless and excited, sir."

"So! The attack may not have been entirely unexpected.

We seem to make a little progress, do we not? Perhaps you would rather do the questioning, Mr. Lestrade?"

"No, Mr. Holmes, it's in better hands than mine."

"Well, we will press on with this note. They wrote it on rough cardboard. Have you any of the sort in the house?"

"I do not think so."

Holmes walked across to the desk and dabbed a little ink from each bottle on to the blotting paper. "They did not print it in this room," he said; "this is black ink and the other purplish. A thick pen did it, and these are fine tipped. No, they did elsewhere it, I should say. Can you make anything of the inscription, Ames?"

"No, sir, nothing."

"What do you think, Mr. Lestrade?"

"It gives me the impression of a secret society of some sort."

"That's my idea, too," said Detective Shore.

"We can adopt it as a working hypothesis and then see how far our difficulties disappear. An agent from such a society makes his way into the house, waits for Dr.

Seward, drains his body of blood, and escapes by climbing down the wall, after leaving a card beside the dead man, which will, when mentioned in the papers, tell other members of the society that vengeance has been done. That all hangs together." Said Holmes.

"That is so, Mr. Holmes."

"Well, unless he has a burrow close by or a change of clothes ready, they can hardly miss him. And yet they HAVE missed him up to now!" Holmes had gone to the window and was examining with his lens the blood mark on the sill. "It is clearly the tread of a foot. It is remarkably narrow; with toes that are longer than the average, the dimensions of a claw, one would say. But what is this under the side table?"

"A loop of flowers, it seems."

"From the garlic plant I suspect."

At that comment, and at some distance from this scene, a pair of sleeping eyes fluttered as ones do during a vivid dream, recalling with delicious memory the glutenous events that they had witnessed only a few hours before.

16

DISCOVER THE UNDEAD DREAM

Can you draw yourself to imagine that the undead dream? I can tell you from what I know now to be true. The time of sleep in any being, living or undead, wrapped tightly with the world of the subconscious mind. Dracula would prove to be no different from any mortal in that respect. The case not yet solved; I bear the ensuing description of evidence found after investigation and prior to the end.

Curving around the innards of a rectangular tower like the body of a coiled cobra ready to strike, scores of narrow steps followed the dark polished handrails down and down further into a darker area. A thin layer of rolling mist clung to the treads like a silent waterfall. Shadows did not live there by choice. Neither did any human or beast of any hope. At the deepest point a heavy wooden door, finished with the same care as the bannisters leading, locked and bolted. As it usually was at a time of daylight.

The door opened into a small windowless room, perhaps more comfortably described as a vault. Its ceiling a solid combination of steel, bolts, panels, and mechanical movement, held still during the hours of darkness. In the center of the room a great wooden box, about double the size and depth of a standard coffin and made more luxurious on its outside. Around it six, slightly smaller and less decorated, boxes. Attached to the exposed brick wall furthest away from the door hung a single flaming torch, flickering in luster and shape as the draft that passed through the space attached itself to the flame. The substance of the floor kept secret by the excess mist flowing through the doorway and settling around the solid objects in its path.

Unlike the others, the largest box had no top or cover. Below the level of the ornate rim, the light from the flame brought to shape the profile of a man's face. Sharp features of the nose and forehead cast withering shadows, which ebbed and then grew with the force of the illumination cast upon them. The appearance was of a man, between death or sleep, resting on a foundation of compacted dark brown earth. Wide open, the eyes were stony, but without the glassiness of death. The color of the cheeks disguised the warmth of life through their pallor. No sign of movement, no pulse, no breath, no beating of the heart. The shiny wax like features held an appearance of cruelty.

It was the Count; it was Dracula, the undead. He lay there looking as if his youth had been half renewed, for the white hair and moustache, as they appeared at his resurrection, now changed to dark grey. The cheeks were full, and the translucent white skin emanated a ruby color from beneath; on the lips were gouts of fresh blood, which, still liquified, trickled from the corners of the mouth and ran over the chin and neck. The deep, burning eyes set amongst swollen flesh, the lids and pouches underneath were bloated. The whole awful creature was simply gorged with blood. He lay like a filthy leech, exhausted with his repletion. There was a mocking smile on the face which recounted the activities of the night before, when he had visited Dr. Seward at Carfax.

In this creature's dream, the images played again and again. His moment of vengeance, the plan coming to form; the eyes remained open, with no movement. The pictures placed him circling the house, undercover of shadow cast by the setting sun. He was waiting for the drawbridge to be raised, and with it the sense of security that it provided for those inside. His entry designed to be the prelude to a horrific encounter. On landing upon the outer wall of the Manor and close to the window of his entry, the sharp claws of his stubby fingers easily imbedded themselves into the soft lime mortar between the brickwork. The window opened without force, a gap narrow enough to allow a shape-shift of his body to pass inside. As he transferred his form, the curtain twitched with the entry of air. He recalled the satisfaction of seeing the look of panic on Dr. Seward's face as he caught in his peripheral vision the demon slowly appear from behind the curtain. Not a draft from the window moving the curtain as he first thought, but the restoring of the lizard into the full personification of the Count.

"Good evening Dr. Seward."

"No, it cannot be you! You are destroyed! I saw it!"

"Well, you can see that is not true. You saw my dust. Dr. the dust that is eternally me. The lifeblood of your fallen friend kindly revived me."

"How can you enter; I have not provided you with the permission that you require? And I demand that you go!"

"Dr. do you not recall, this is my property, I purchased it over seven years since, I need no permission. As you may now recall from my previous visits to you these past few weeks, you have provided good sustenance. But that is done and now is the end."

The Count's eyes reddened, and his brows raised themselves as a single line across his forehead. Seward grabbed into his dressing gown pocket and found the crucifix within but could not release it. At the same time the hand of the Count struck out and held the Dr. by the throat, lifting him off his feet, which now dangled above the floor without control. Power and darkness flowed through Seward's body from the Count. His grip on the crucifix strengthened, not to gain or receive relief, but to twist and scorch its shape against the skin of his palm. Seward's eyes had the look of fear, glancing at the side table beside his bed and the bundle of white flowers upon it.

Dracula, still holding Seward's neck in his single hand, followed the glance. "Those are no good to you now, my friend."

Seward let out a muffled murmur, only a whisper. A cry for help not heard as Dracula threw the neck to be exposed and set his mouth firmly on the jugular and took a long steady feed. The body became limp and the glow from the skin disappeared as if someone had turned the light within off. Dracula released his grip, and the contorted remains fell in a heap on the floor. Seward's blood dribbled down the Count's lips and neck.

"Now, Mr. Holmes, a note for your interest."

Dracula took from his pocket a scrap of paper and dropped it beside the curtain as he wrapped himself in his cape and shape-shifted out of the window. Not requiring the use of the drawbridge, ladder, rope, or any contact with the ground to return to his lair in the heart of London.

17

A DREADFUL REALIZATION

For now, there were no further clues or questions to be had at the Carfax Estate. We left the investigation in the capable hands of Inspector Lestrade. The murder of Dr. Seward had engaged Sherlock in a line of thought and investigation that he warranted never to consider. Some form of supernatural intervention and a dreadful realization that this could be the fact.

A fact that he was fighting against with all of his logical mind. His face bore the puzzle upon it as we left the village and walked to the station. We caught the first available train from Purfleet. The first part of the journey begun in silence, Sherlock lost in thought, staring out of the window, until he said.

"The tragedy has been so uncommon, so complete and of such personal importance to so many people, that we are suffering from a plethora of surmise, conjecture, and hypothesis. The difficulty is to detach the framework of fact, of absolute undeniable fact, from the embellishments of theorists and soon reporters. Then, having established ourselves upon this sound basis, it is our duty to see what inferences may be drawn and what are the special points upon which the complete mystery turns."

Ten minutes later the train pulled into Victoria, and we were both in a cab and rattling through the streets on our way back to Baker Street. At points I caught a view of the faint halo of the sun as it appeared between the silhouettes of the buildings. The swirling dirty yellow fog obscuring their full form as they grasped upwards for the sight of a clear sky. We hurried on, seeing the occasional figures of citizens as we passed them, blurred and indistinct in the opalescent London reek. Holmes nestled in silence into his heavy coat, and I was glad to do the same, for the air was most bitter, both in temperature and odor.

We Settled back into the apartment; it was not until we had consumed a pot of hot tea prepared to perfection by Mrs. Hudson that Sherlock became re-energized by the whole affair. Although not showing the same, as he sat in his big armchair with the weary, heavy-lidded expression which veiled his eager nature. I noted the time from the clock on the mantle. It was just before eleven.

"Watson, any news in the Gazette this morning of the Purfleet Mystery, what of the headline?"

I picked up the newspaper from its usual spot on the table, and as one would do, read the headline aloud. Sherlock was sitting in his armchair with his long fingertips pressed together. Unusually, he was interested and concentrating upon my words.

"The newly opened Tower Bridge, a haven for criminals, it says. This new and impressive centerpiece of the nation's capital, so pleasantly welcomed into use by the Prince and Princess of Wales in June of this year, has become the unfortunate home for the mischievous and criminal minded of the area.

The bridge, in construction for over eight years prior to its opening, has proven to be a welcome resource for the most unsavory class of person. Spanning the width of the river, the overhead walkways, some two hundred and seventy feet, join the towers. Designed to allow pedestrians to cross when the bridge is raised. The walkways have now become hangouts for prostitutes and thieves. There are many pleas to clear the pathways of such users before they become permanent dwellings for the underbelly of our society."

"Presently Watson, I do not need to retain such information other than the bridge provides a welcome crossing from Southwark to Whitechapel; and that it is better to pass by cab than by foot. Then nothing of the Purfleet Mystery says you?"

"None that I have found Sherlock."

"Then we must return to our priority. What of the note, Watson?"

"Oh, well yes, the cipher. I have it here. 5-5-62, 5-5-57, OR, 28-5-644, 25-6-269, D."

"Now, pull the journal and the letter from Harker that contains the original coding. Make a note of the numbers and pass the scrap to me for examination."

I set out Harker's journal and found the word for each part of the cipher while Sherlock compared the two writings, holding one in each hand.

"I have it Holmes, SLEEP AWAKE OR PLEASURE DEATH D, that is the message, but what of its meaning?"

"The 'D' is evidently Dracula. I have compared the notes. The handwriting, pen and ink used to scribe them are remarkably different. The first is definitively of Harker's hand, the other must be of the Count. He comes after them all, Watson. That is the meaning, he warns us he will attend to this business during the hours of darkness."

"All of them?" That was the dreadful realization. I realized this was a case of a planned vengeance against those who had sought Dracula's extinction.

"Yes, my good friend, Seward was the first. Then there is Godalming, Van Helsing, and the Harker's, Jonathan, Mina and their son Quincy. In that order I fashion."

"But how is Dracula to know the key to the cipher?"

"That is yet another mystery to be solved. First, we must send a telegram to Van Helsing. Contact Mina and get his address. Somewhere in Amsterdam I know. Then we must locate Godalming, before the day is out."

"If he is not in London, then he will be at his residence in Exeter."

The telegram to Mina returned an address for Van Helsing in a matter of hours. I sent the following message to Amsterdam before we left for Exeter early that afternoon.

Telegram to Abraham Van Helsing, M. D., D. Ph., D. Lit.

Dr. Seward murdered. Need your help. Come presently 221B Baker Street.

Sherlock Holmes.

"We have just time to catch our train at Paddington, and I will go further into the matter upon our journey. You would oblige me by bringing with you all the journals in our possession."

And so, an hour later I found myself in the corner of a first-class carriage flying along en-route for Exeter, while Sherlock Holmes, with his sharp, eager face framed in his ear-flapped travelling-cap, dipped rapidly into the bundle of journals. We had left Reading far behind us before he thrust the last one of them onto the table between us and offered me his cigarette-case.

“I think you know me well enough, Watson, to understand that I am not a nervous man. It is stupidity rather than courage to refuse to recognize danger when it is close upon you. Might I trouble you for a match?”

He drew in the smoke of his cigarette as if the soothing influence were grateful to him. There was something strange about all this. It was not Holmes’s nature to be so concerned, and something about his now pale, drawn face told me that his nerves were at their highest tension. He saw the question in my eyes, and, putting his fingertips together and his elbows upon the table, he explained the situation.

“As you are aware, Watson, there is no one who knows the higher criminal world of London, so well as I do. For years past I have continually been conscious of some power behind the malefactor, some deep organizing power which forever stands in the law’s way and throws its shield over the wrongdoer.

Again, and again in cases of the most varying sorts, kidnappings, disappearances, robberies, and murders, I have felt this force, and I have deduced its action in many of those undiscovered crimes in which they have not consulted me. For years I have endeavored to break through the veil which shrouded it, until the murder of Dr. Seward, led me, after a thousand cunning windings, to confirm that power is Dracula."

The evening was drawing in when we reached Exeter. Holmes was very serious in his manner and myself. I was scared, if not curious.

18

HORROR IN EXETER

It was that evening that all London became interested, and the fashionable world dismayed, on hearing the news of the murder of Dr. Seward under the most unusual and inexplicable circumstances. All as I have mentioned previously. The public learned some details of the crime which came out in the press release issued by the police. However, a good deal of what Sherlock proposed suppressed, or possibly more remarkably ignored. If the wider population knew of the monster that was at large and at their windows while they slept, it would surely cause the utmost fright and panic in the streets.

"The newspapers have the Purfleet Mystery." I said, after glancing at the headlines of the evening editions bound and stockpiled on a newspaper stand as we walked at a determined pace out of the station.

"Then we better solve this thing before it travels to a darker place. We must hurry our arrival to the Godalming residence. The light of the sun is losing its bearing on this dull day." Said Sherlock.

"At least we can catch a view of the giver of light now we are far from the confines of those dank London streets." I replied.

We left the station in a cab and made haste to the residence, which was located some distance from the station on Baring Crescent and a point beyond the center of town. We approached the destination at a trot twenty minutes after leaving the station. There, at the end of the row, stood a grand white rendered detached Victorian home of three floors above a basement. All the windows disclosed a calming amber light from the interior, which put a subdued illumination upon the landscaping below their openings. The main entrance door was set on the right of the building, within its own porch.

“We are in luck Sherlock; they are at home.”

The cab stopped at the end of the short carriageway to the front door. We approached together and with a firm hand Sherlock knocked twice on the dark glossy panels, before pulling at the bell ring. The door opened immediately, and a young maid stood with a welcoming smile to greet us.

“Hello, I am Sherlock Holmes and I need to speak urgently with Lord Godalming.”

“Sorry Sir, he is not at home at this moment.”

“Then where will he be this hour, do you know?”

“He is attending the Royal in town with Lady Godalming. It is the showing of Mary Shelley’s Frankenstein. A most shocking affair by most accounts.”

We returned to the cab and instructed the driver to take us to the venue at speed. It would take no longer than ten minutes at the most. The Theatre Royal, on the corner of Longbrook Street and New North Road, was a significant landmark in town, but had a tragic history. In September 1887, a fire had taken hold of the original building and in a matter of moments, panic broke out as the flames spread. The building destroyed. There were over one-hundred and eighty victims. Many from the upper gallery who could not escape because of poorly designed exits. Tonight, the performance of Mary Shelley's Frankenstein would bring an interested audience. The number in attendance would be substantial.

It was not yet five o'clock; the day had been a dreary one, and a dense drizzly fog lay low upon the streets of Exeter. Dull clouds, made duller by the ending of whatever light the sun had brought, drooped sadly over the muddy streets. Down Longbrook Street, the lamps were but misty splotches of diffused light which threw a feeble circular glimmer upon the slimy pavement. The yellow glow from the shop windows streamed out into the steamy, vaporous air, and threw a murky, shifting radiance across the crowded thoroughfare. There was, to my mind, something eerie and ghost-like in the endless procession of faces which flitted across these narrow bars of light, sad faces and glad, haggard, and merry. Like all humankind, they flitted from the gloom into the light, and so back into the misery once more. I am not subject to impressions, but the dull, heavy evening, with the strange business upon which we were engaged, combined to make me nervous and depressed. Holmes alone could rise superior to petty influences and remained in wonderful spirit, eager to visit with Godalming.

At the Theatre Royal, the crowds were already thick at the side-entrances. In front a continuous stream of hansoms and four-wheelers were rattling up, discharging their cargoes of shirt-fronted men and bediamonded women. We had hardly reached past the main entrance before a small, dark, rustic man in the dress of a doorman accosted us as we made our way past the ticket office into the lobby.

"Do you have a ticket, sir?"

"No, I do not. We are here on a matter of some urgency. A man's life is in danger. And that man is inside this Theatre."

"You are the police then, sir?"

"No, I am Sherlock Holmes, and this is my good friend Dr. Watson."

"That is very well, sir. I cannot let you in without a ticket. It is the rule."

"Well, the rule, and your implementation of it, may cause the death of one of your patrons!"

Sherlock, increasingly frustrated with the argument in

front of him, turned on his heels and maneuvered me with him back onto the street, then in front and then towards the performers' entrance on the side of the building.

"We will make our own entrance, Watson!"

Sherlock pulled from his pocket a set of skeleton keys, which he carried at all times. One of his skills was that of a master locksmith. No locked door had proved to be an obstacle to his progress. I shielded him as he worked on the lock. The keys rattling against each other until the bolt gave the satisfying click of submission. We entered the interior of the Theatre, evidently at a point within a corridor and prop area backstage of the main auditorium. The performance would start in a matter of minutes. Stagehands, actors, and scenery passed before us as we considered our location. Sherlock grabbed a great piece of board shaped like a tree and motioned for me to hold on to the other end. We carried it, concealing ourselves as part of the production team, and ended at the right side of the stage, behind the side curtain.

"Watson, we have an excellent view of the auditorium and balconies from this vantage. Quickly scan them for a sight of Godalming."

"But we do not know his appearance, Sherlock!"

"He is a Lord. Look for the understated but opulent dress of such!"

We scanned the faces of the audience, but the lighting had already dimmed and it was almost impossible to make out any features, never mind how they dressed. Suddenly, as we continued in our task, there was a terrifying high-pitched scream of a woman's voice from a balcony to our left.

As we both turned towards the voice, so did most of the audience. Then two gunshots rang out in quick fashion, one coming after the other from the same point. The flashes of the projectiles as they left the muzzle of the pistol illuminating the balcony and the figures upon it. Silhouettes within a struggle. Momentarily, some parts of the Theatre brightened as the escape lighting activated. The performance became silent, as did the audience. All eyes moved towards the balcony.

Two men struggled against each other. Although it seemed in appearance a strange sort of dance. Their torso's twisting back and forth. One bending the other backwards and leaning close into the throat. The spotlight operator focused on the struggle and highlighted the men as they paused and stood together, motionless, for a few moments. Still illuminated by the bright light, the face of the one with the upper hand turned and looked against the eyes that held him in view.

It was a tremendously virile and yet sinister face which was turned towards us. With the brow of a philosopher above and the jaw of a sensualist below. One could not look upon his cruel red eyes, with their drooping, cynical lids, or upon the fierce, aggressive nose and the sinister, deep-lined brow, without reading Nature's plainest danger-signals. He took no heed of us. But the monster's eyes were fixed upon Holmes' face with an expression in which hatred and acknowledgement were equally blended.

"It is him It is Dracula!" Sherlock muttered.

The Count lifted the drained, now lifeless body of Godalming with one hand and raised it above his head with such ease that the audience gasped. Some thinking that this was part of the show. Dracula tilted his head in a theatrical signal of victory before throwing the limp cadaver from the balcony into the seating below. The spotlight operator tracked the descent of the body. The screams of the audience and actors alike were followed by the sickening sound of breaking backbone as a handrail halted its fall. All then realized that this was no theatrical show, but a vicious life taking attack.

Sherlock leapt from the corner of the stage towards the fallen corpse of the man. It was Godalming; I followed two steps behind. The body lay twisted over the rail, the same look on the white face as we had seen on Seward's, of horror and fright. The twin circular puncture marks upon the jugular made fresh by the attack dripped with whatever remnant of blood remained inside, and by judging from the waxy pallor of the skin was almost none. Sherlock carried out a quick examination of the clothing and the hands, flitting around the body with intent only known to himself.

"There is nothing to be done with this man now. Quick, to the balcony."

As all eyes in the Theatre had focused on the body and its fall, no one had observed how and where Dracula had escaped, or even if he was still on the balcony above. We found the stairs and rushed to the door of the box. A crowd had gathered around Lady Godalming, who had screamed and then fainted at the commencement of the attack. A pistol lay on the floor. Sherlock picked it up using a pencil from his pocket and sniffed the barrel. As he replaced it carefully on the spot from where it came, he noticed a scrap of paper. Another cipher. He gathered the message up in his palm before anyone noticed. His attention turned to the walls of the balcony behind the direction of where Dracula had appeared. On close examination he found two holes, similar to those he generated himself in the apartment when he took to indoor target practice. He took out his pocket-knife and dug into the hole, releasing a bullet, which he deposited into his handkerchief, wrapping it carefully before returning the entire package to his jacket.

"We need to inform Lestrade of Scotland Yard at once, but we must return to Baker Street by morning to hear of any return of message from Van Helsing. He too is in danger; we must also warn Mina and Jonathan."

19

DRAMA IN THE THEATRE

The local police were soon in attendance and ushered the audience out of the Theatre Royal at its main entrance and onto the damp and foggy street. The disgorged patrons gathered tightly together, and by their congregation, unwilling to disperse, formed a shadow of a crocodile. A rowdy group spilling from the adjacent New London Inn, and having a loud inquisitiveness amongst themselves, reinforced the crowd. Each person milling around their own space, relaying the tale of the attack to their neighbor. Speaking of the terrible fall and sound of death that was still in their ears. With such a headline ready to print, it would not be long before the local press would find this event and circle the Theatre like buzzards for the story. The constables secured the area, creating a slim pathway to the main entrance, a mouth to the crocodile. The local detectives moved in, squeezing through the crowd to be swallowed by the Theatre entrance.

First to the scene was inspector George Barton, a sturdy, middle-sized fellow, some thirty years of age, clean-shaven, and sallow skinned, with a bland, insinuating manner, and a pair of wonderfully sharp and penetrating grey eyes. Inspector Barton, who had charge of the case, made, in his mind, a very careful examination of the balcony area and around the fallen body of the late Lord laying in the auditorium.

He found nothing which he thought could throw any light upon the matter and already made the conclusion. He shot a questioning glance at each of us, and with a slight bow sidled down into the nearest chair beside Sherlock as he stood against the same rail which the Lord had fallen.

"Now gentlemen, I am Inspector Barton of the Devon Constabulary, and I hope you do not mind answering a few questions."

"Not at all, Inspector, but wouldn't you want to know what happened here as a priority?"

"First things first, can I have your names?" Sherlock spun away in hopeless disgust, and I stepped forward to head off the petulant response waiting at his lips.

"I'm Dr. Watson and this is my friend Sherlock Holmes."

"Ah, the famous amateur, we have it solved then! I am informed by the doorman that you had knowledge of the crime prior to it being committed. How so?"

"Have you seen a copy of this evening's press inspector, the article about the Purfleet Mystery perchance?"

"Can't say that I have. Why? Is it of some importance to this case? I have undertaken a thorough investigation of the scene and have found nothing which carries me against thinking that the Lord was murdered. Being thrown from the balcony, breaking his back from the fall. That causing his death. Naturally!"

"Naturally? My dear fellow, I find it utterly disturbing that the lack of experience and knowledge that you have accumulated removes care about the finer shades of analysis and deduction! But if you are trivial, I cannot blame you, for the days of the exceptional cases are past. Man, or at least criminal man, has lost all enterprise and originality."

"Says you Mr. Holmes."

"Yes, says I. What of the man lying there with a broken back? He was at least unconscious as he fell, if not already dead. There is not a thimble of blood in his system. It has all been drained. Did you examine the two small puncture marks upon the jugular? Where did it go?"

"He may be anemic, or surely have some other medical condition."

They now knew that Lady Godalming had fainted at the sight of the Count as he entered the box, and the police escorted her home in a cab, as her presence could be of no help to them in their investigations.

"Also, Godalming shot at the murderer at least twice. All eyes in the Theatre, apart from the dear fainted Lady, who was unconscious and splayed upon the balcony floor, witnessed the attack and ensuing struggle. The Lord could not have missed at such close range."

"It is possible, though! Is it not?"

"Yes, it is possible. But unlikely."

"But, why on earth would the Lord need to carry a gun to the Theatre?"

"He knew, just as I, that he was in danger."

"But if a man had a danger hanging over him, and knew what it was, do not you think he would turn to the police for protection?"

"Maybe it was some danger that he could not be protected against. Look at this. Here is one bullet that I pulled from the wall." Sherlock removed his handkerchief complete with the bullet that he had collected earlier, unwrapped it, handing to Barton by laying it in the inspector's left palm. He then handed Barton his eyeglass, which the inspector attempted to focus on the lead.

"Please examine the tip inspector."

"I see, but what am I looking for here?"

"You will observe at the tip the bullet embedded threads of material that are not present within the wall from which I extracted it, mostly plaster and paper. Small threads of dark cloth. Similar to, if not the, clothing worn by the attacker, yet there is no blood spilled on the balcony floor. Did the bullet pass through the attacker?"

"There's no flesh attached."

"Maybe there was none to attach to."

"This bullet obviously missed its target then."

"Or the target had no substance that could affect the projectile."

"That cannot be the case, Mr. Holmes, a remarkable supposition you propose. I suggest you leave the detective work to those who know it. We are not on the busy streets of Soho now! I think that you have nothing more to add here, Mr. Holmes. If I need more answers, I shall contact you."

"Quite so, inspector." Said Sherlock, pulling at the front of his cap and smiling at the inspector extremely condescendingly.

"Let us return to London on the night train Watson, we have nothing more to gain, or to offer, from attending this scene."

"But..."

"But nothing Watson. To the cab, my good fellow."

A ride to the station delivered us to a wait of twenty minutes for the night train to London. Sherlock did not utter a single word until the moment that we were to board, then as we were seated in a carriage to ourselves, said:

"You carry the journals with you, Watson?"

"Yes, right here in my satchel."

"You witnessed the incompetence! I have no hope that the locals there will pull anything of consequence. We shall decode the message and then pass the findings of my examination of the scene onto Lestrade for further investigation. From first examination it is of the same paper and ink that we found at Carfax."

"What of the cipher?" Sherlock handed me the scrap of paper that carried the following inscription. '4-5-88! 30-6-34, NOW, 15-5-2, 8-5-325, 17-5-36, 12-5-5 D'

"The D shows it may be from Dracula. However, I am still in the dark about how the Count knows of the cipher and can send messages like such!" I said.

“First, decode the message and I shall reveal the solution. It sits in the journals that we have in hand.”

I pulled the journal of Jonathan Harker from the satchel and set about the message as the train continued onward.

“We both know the reason for what we witnessed tonight. Dracula is carrying out a plan of revenge. A carefully choreographed sequence of pre-arranged attacks. There can be no delay here. It is most important that we keep as close a step to Dracula as is possible.”

20

FINDING

It was early Wednesday morning, and the darkness was on the edge of breaking when the train arrived at Paddington. The station was readying itself for the industry of the day, trains being brought to steam and the bustle of men loading freight and bags of mail. Large wooden boxes of all sizes carried on carts to the wagons. Our first sight of the morning papers had the headline, 'Murder at the cursed Exeter Theatre.'

I picked up a copy and hailed a cab, stretching to meet Sherlock's strides as he hurried on. Outside, the new day opening for business, the clinging ochre mist, holding the excrement of the atmosphere, complementing the slate gray rooftops. In the ten minutes that it took to return to Baker Street, normal daytime activity had resumed. Horses, carts, the bustle of commerce, the noise of human endeavor and the putrid smell of horse waste compacted into the roadway. Business as usual, no-one had a care of what happened in Exeter. Why should they? No-one connected with the death of Dr. Seward other than Sherlock and me. The moment that we were back in the apartment, Sherlock was eager to discuss the issues at hand.

It had been only a matter of a few days since Mina Harker visited us and engaged in this awful tale. It had led us without respite to two murders and with seemingly more to come. The travels and events had exhausted us both physically, but the whole affair entirely energized Sherlock's mental capacity.

"Tell me the solution to the cipher Watson, if you, have it?"

"I will Sherlock, then for my sake, retire for a moment's sleep. Here, I have it. The cipher decodes to FRIGHTENED! DEATH NOW MORE COMING UNQUESTIONABLE FACTS. D."

"Do you feel a creeping, shrinking sensation, Watson, when you read this? Is it the same feeling when you stand before the legless reptiles in the Zoo, and see the slithery, gliding, venomous creatures, with their deadly lifeless eyes and wicked, flattened faces? Well, that's how Dracula set himself into my senses. I have had to do with fifty murderers in my career, but the worst of them never gave me the repulsion which I have for this fellow. The look of hatred in those eyes could pierce the strongest man. It is clear from the message that he expects us to be in fear but knows well that the track that we are on is the right one. Take some sleep, Watson, but be quick about it for we have a lot to question today."

Sleep I made, but I awoke after a restless two-hours, disturbed by the visions of last night's horrific murder of Lord Godalming and the memory of Dr. Seward's contorted face. I could not shake them, because there was no rational explanation for either.

I returned to the lounge with a feverish complexion about me. Sherlock was sitting hunched over his microscope, surrounded with bottles, papers and test-tubes. The day was now as bright as it would become, but the room was in darkness save for the lamp that sat in front of Holmes as he considered and made a note of his discoveries.

"Watson, here you are. Take a seat and ready yourself for my findings of this morning."

"May I let some light in this place before we do so? The darkness in this room does nothing to render my mood in the right direction." I requested.

At the very moment I drew the curtains back as far as they would travel, there was a knock at the front door at the street. Footsteps on the stairs and then, with no fanfare, Mrs. Hudson ushering in Inspector Lestrade.

"Lestrade! Just the man that we need, and right on time!" Sherlock roared.

"I heard the news from Exeter Sherlock. Lord Godalming, did he not have a connection with Seward? Over the Dracula tale that we heard relayed by Mrs. Harker?"

"Yes, my good fellow, he did, and he has paid that price."

"You, know more detail about these events?"

"Yes, I think I may. Now, gentlemen," said my friend gravely, "I am asking you now to put everything to the test with me, and you will judge for yourselves whether the observations I have made justify the conclusions to which I have come."

Sherlock took his pipe and lit it. After a couple of quick draws of air, a cloud of hazy brown tobacco smoke blew across the room. He then removed himself from the table and slumped into his chair. The leather squealing under his weight. I took my seat, and Lestrade sat in the remaining chair between the two of us.

"The first I have to speak to relates to the notes of poor Dr. Seward. The entry of 11th September has some relevance here. If you would Watson take the journal."

I opened Dr. Seward's diary at the entry and read the first paragraph openly to the others:

'11 September. - This afternoon I went over to Hillingham. Found Van Helsing in excellent spirits, and Lucy much better. Shortly after I had arrived, a big parcel from abroad came for the Professor. He opened it with much impressment—assumed, of course—and showed a great bundle of white flowers.'

"The garlic flowers, Sherlock?"

"Yes, Watson, those white flowers. Do you not recall that in the room where Dr. Seward found horribly slain, under the side table a small bunch of white flowers?"

"Yes, I recall!" Lestrade shouted.

"When I smelled the clothing of Seward, there was a mixture of two distinct aromas, garlic being one."

"The other?"

"The other, the acidic scent of citrus."

"Citrus?"

"Yes, Lestrade, let us revisit your visit to Dracula's office those years ago. I asked whether there was an arrangement of citrus fruit in the room. You recalled that there was a bowl of grapefruit."

"Yes, so I did because there was. What is the importance there?"

"Sodium citrate."

"What is that?"

"Sodium citrate is used to prevent blood from clotting in storage. It is also used in a laboratory, before an operation, to determine whether blood is too thick and might cause a blood clot, or if the blood is too thin to operate safely. The substance used in the surgery of animals for many years. There are studies, not yet published on its use in humans."

"My word, Holmes. The Count was feeding his victims this substance through citrus fruits to thin their blood!" I said sharply.

"Yes, this is how he withdraws the volume of blood in the time during his attack. But there is a question remaining."

"This is already too fanciful for my mind, Sherlock. Again, you leave me behind with your analysis. But what is outstanding here?" Lestrade spoke, shaking his head in disbelief.

"The question being, how did the Count get to Exeter, some three hours travelling from London, in time to conceal himself in the Theatre last night? And why did the shots fired by Godalming cause no harm to the attacker?"

21

RETURN TO THE LAIR

Sherlock leapt to his feet and took a few more shallow puffs of his pipe, in exchange exhaling more clouds of putrid smelling vapor ahead of his direction, like a steam train charging through a tunnel. He was in deep thought regarding the likely whereabouts of the lair that Dracula would require in order to carry out these horrific deeds without discovery. And from which location he was garnering help. Lestrade and I remained seated as Holmes paced back and forth, his brow furrowed in weight of the mental exertions beneath.

"From the experiences of Jonathan Harker, when held in the Count's castle, Dracula will have set himself quarters to meet his needs. A place kept in darkness during the daylight hours. Somewhere that would be undiscovered other than by chance. But what of these needs?"

"I would say Holmes that the last time he was in London was at the Carfax estate. My thinking would be that he has set himself in a grand, remote place outside the purview of humanity."

"Not this time Watson, that was his downfall, was it not? His searchers easily found him, those looking to cause him harm. He will surely not make that same mistake. It would need to be close to the center of London, secure and unobtrusive. Somewhere that a sparsity of daytime activity would not be unusual enough to draw attention."

"But yet, that is like looking for the needle, Sherlock."

Notwithstanding the discussion occurring in the room of 221B Baker Street, there were at the same time other events that we came to discover these facts, which were not familiar to us until later in the investigation. I report them in order of this case to confine the events to a logical timeline.

Four men, one at each corner, carried a box between them at shoulder height. The box itself was a solid timber crate the length of a man and one and a half times his width. The men, poorly dressed, mostly in black cloth that hung off their emaciated and pale bodies, stepped in time with each other as though under command. Their path taken with care down the spiral staircase described earlier, carrying the box at a height that avoided the bannisters, enough to steady it in a horizontal plane. It was the same staircase that led to the lair of Dracula. The heavy wooden door held secure until they approached, then without asking for a key, the door opened, and the men and box entered the room.

Their journey had started the previous day when they had collected the same goods from the very spot that they would return. The open cart in which the box was first laid carried it, together with a variety of others, different sizes and weights, through the crowded streets of London.

The men deposited their conveyance at Paddington train station to be taken to Exeter on the early afternoon mail wagon. They took tickets to travel as passengers on the same train. On arrival at Exeter, after unloading the box and securing appropriate transportation, they established that Lord Godalming would visit the Theatre that very evening. Before the venue had opened, the men had successfully deposited their cargo within the back-stage area of the Theatre.

It was from there after sunset that Dracula had emerged and tracked Godalming and his wife to the fateful balcony box, hiding in the dark recess behind a hanging wall covering. He waited with all patience until the performance had started and the auditorium lights dimmed. Then he threw the covering to one side and instantly met with the gaze of Lady Godalming. His red eyes struck her with such fear and horror that she screamed as the Count placed her in a hypnotic state so that she fell to the ground in a heap. Lord Godalming turned to face the monster he last saw shrink to a pile of dust some seven years earlier in the Carpathian Mountains.

"No, you..."

"Yes, it is me, no mistake my good Lord, I am here to take from you what you tried to take from me."

At that moment Godalming drew his pistol from his side and aimed it at the Count's heart. Since his first encounter with the Count, Godalming had always carried a pistol. Not because he ever thought that this day would come, but because he knew that there was unexplained evil in this world. Godalming smiled as he pointed the gun and set his finger on the trigger.

"I have you, do not move or I shall let you have it with no remorse."

Dracula lunged forward with outstretched arms; he was only two steps distant from the Lord. The gun fired, twice in quick succession, before he took hold of his prey, with one hand gripping the neck. The bullets did not miss; they entered their target and passed through, both rounds lodging in the wall beyond. In any mortal being such aim and damage would have rendered the attacker immobile if not immediately dead.

But this was no mortal. There was no living flesh beneath the clothing. He continued without delay. Illuminated by the Theatre spotlight, the struggle was quickly over. There was not enough strength in Godalming to prevent him from being overpowered. The victim now limp, Dracula took his fill from the jugular, held up the drained body and threw it from the balcony into the seating below. The chaos within the Theatre, with patrons running for the exits, covered his tracks as he made his way to the box, which was collected as soon as the police vacated the premises.

After the deed was done, they repeated the journey in reverse, returning the contents to the point of origination. They deposited the box alongside the largest container within the center of the room and the top carefully removed. Inside lay the now youthful form of the Count, the hair, and the eyebrows reinvigorated to the darkest black and the skin lively with the undercurrent of fresh nutrition. The men lifted the rigid body and laid it within its preferred resting place.

Directly next to the large box, one of the six previously sealed smaller containers was now free from its lid and held a form. A familiar face, less contorted now than we had last seen, and seemingly more at rest. The flesh sunken and having a sallow pallor about it added an age to the features. The eyes open, caught between life and death, stared at the ceiling of the room with no movement. It was a man, not now human, but converted through his death at the hands of Dracula, to the existence of a vampire commanded by his master.

It was the same day that an article in the Gazette called

out mysterious events of the night before, which brought a similarity to events reported seven years prior. Here follows an extract from the article:

'A SOUTHWARK PARK MYSTERY.

The neighborhood of Bermondsey is just at present exercised with a series of events which seem to run-on lines parallel to those of what we knew to be the "HAMSTEAD MYSTERY". Reported some seven years since. During the past two days several cases have occurred of young children straying from home or neglecting to return from their playing in the Southwark Park. In all these cases the children were too young to give any properly intelligible account of themselves, but the consensus of their excuses is that they had been with a "doctor man."

It has always been late in the evening when they are missed, and on two occasions they have not found the children until early in the following morning. It is supposed in the neighborhood that, as the first child missed gave as his reason for being away that a "doctor man" had asked him to come for a walk, the others had picked up the phrase and used it as occasion served. This is the more natural as the favorite game of the little ones at present is luring each other away by wiles.

In an obscure coincidence, all who have been missed at night have been slightly torn or wounded in the throat. The puncture marks seem as a small animal may have made them. Such as the fox that caused havoc with the wild fowl in the same park only four years ago. Although of not much importance individually, the wounds would show that whatever animal inflicts them has a system or method of its own. I have instructed the police of the division to keep a sharp look-out for wandering children, especially when very young, in and around Southwark Park, and for any stray fox which may be about.'

Now, our thoughts turned to Dracula and whatever help he may have gathered since his return to London, and to the more likely whereabouts of his lair.

22

EXCHANGE OF CORRESPONDENCE

"My dear fellows," said Sherlock Holmes as he rejoined Lestrade and myself and slumped back in his chair, moving it backwards with the force of his landing. Leaning forward, he placed his hands together, fingertips firmly against their opposite number. As was his position in time of thought. We were then all sitting in front of the fire in silence, gazing into it as it released a rising stream of glowing embers, fading into the darkness of the chimney that they fed. A warm light emanated from the source and spread through the apartment at Baker Street. Our animated shadows fell on the wall behind as we recommenced the discussion of the case. Sherlock opened his thoughts to us both. “Life is infinitely stranger than anything which the mind of man could invent, do you not think?”

Two murders by a being with so greater darkness around him that one would have thought, without seeing firsthand, could not exist. We would not dare to conceive the things which are really mere commonplaces of existence. If we could fly out of that window hand in hand, hover over this great city, gently remove the roofs, and peep in at the most obscure things which are going on, leading to the most startling results, it would make all fiction with its conventionalities and foreseen conclusions most stale and unprofitable.”

“That maybe the case,” said Lestrade, “but it appears most likely that such a demon, a real and tangible demon, exists within a range of us. As you have seen with your own eyes. You cannot now doubt it. Why other would we search for his lair, you are with us on that track?”

“And there are the journals, written by individual hand. There can surely be no denying that Dracula is imbued with certain remarkable powers.” Said I. At that moment, the door burst wide open, and we all looked to meet the familiar intruder flying at speed towards Sherlock.

“Sherlock, you have a telegram, from Europe!” Said Mrs. Hudson as she closed upon Holmes with the abandonment and excitement of a young scholar, as if she had never seen correspondence from a foreign land before. She hung about Sherlock as he opened the note, standing on tiptoe and peering over his shoulder as he examined the envelope.

“Thank you, Mrs. Hudson. A response from Professor Van Helsing I expect, telling of his arrival, and at precisely at the best moment to add to our investigation.” Sherlock, as usual, was correct in his prediction. He read the contents so we and Mrs. Hudson could hear:

“Telegram: Sherlock Holmes, 221B Baker Street London England.”

“Such terrible news. This is greatest worry. I shall be in London at the end of this week. Be careful.”

“Professor Van Helsing.”

“We need to be in here to meet with the Professor on his

arrival in two days, as I know he has a vital role in the solving of this mystery and has experience in the apprehension of Dracula. But for now, we will visit with the Harker's."

"They are, as you know, Sherlock living in Whitby. There is no method known to man that would deliver us there and back in under three days!"

"That maybe so, my dear Watson. You are correct in your calculations, the journey by train is not direct and would take the most part of an entire day to reach that destination. And, as you know at our last discussion before we journeyed to Purfleet on that horrific night, I promised Mina I would visit with her this week. From my observations, I realized we may not need to travel too far to do so. This confirmed itself by subsequent events and circumstances. Watson, please telegraph the Great Western Railway hotel, where we left Mina at Victoria that night. The message should read:"

"Telegram: Jonathan & Mina Harker, Care of the Great Western Railway Hotel

Visit 221B Baker Street. News is not good. Take preventative measures. Urgent.

Sherlock Holmes."

“How do you know that Mina and Jonathan are in that hotel, Sherlock?”

“I have a notion that they always planned that Mina would stay in London.”

“What logic brings you to that, Holmes?”

“Elementary Watson, if you recall, when the young lady arrived at our door that night, the only luggage she held with her was a carpetbag. It carried nothing more than the journals she was to deliver to us. Her clothing, neatly pressed and did not show the creases that any dress would having journeyed for at least two days before her arrival in London from Whitby. There were no signs of soot and no aroma of smoke from being carried in a coach behind the engine, as most travelers suffer. Her shoes bore the materials from her hometown and not from the streets of London. Therefore, she must have changed her outfit, before her visit to our apartment.”

“Remarkable, quite remarkable, Homes.” Said Lestrade, adding. “But that does not explain why you placed them in that hotel.”

“Think of our journey that night to Victoria on the news of

the murder of Seward. Mina had said that she had arrived from Whitby that night and would return to her home the next day. In most circumstances and in pursuing easier living, people locate themselves closest to the point of arrival and departure. Mina made no protest at being dropped at the hotel nearest to Victoria."

"That being the station then Holmes." I added.

"Not so fast Watson. Travel by rail to the Northeast originates from the station at St. Pancras, not therefore from Victoria. Mina had positioned herself there because she somehow knew or had information prior to her visit that we would journey to Victoria before we would have done so. She had positioned herself accordingly."

"You think she was aware of the matter at Carfax? But have you thought of an immediate danger overshadowing the Harker's, Sherlock?"

"Yes, Watson. There is no doubt in my mind that they and Professor Van Helsing are the next in line as the targets of Dracula and his plan of revenge. It matters not where they are. All those remaining of the six who ambushed the Count's transport those years ago are in immediate danger. He has shown that he will take payment from each with their lives. We must inform all of them of what we have witnessed. Yet, I do not understand the order of his attacks, or whether there is any order in them at all. He has taken two. Four remain."

"You say four remain Sherlock, but the Gypsies killed Quincy Jones in the venture as you know, some years past at that."

"Yes, Watson, but now there is a namesake replacement, in the form of Quincy Harker, the son."

Sherlock stopped for a moment, considering his thought. "We know Mina has led a most quiet and respectable life in Whitby for the last seven years. She has hardly been away from her home for a day during that time. Why on earth should she choose to travel to London and then arrive on our doorstep that night, especially as, unless she is a most consummate actress, she understands as little of the matter as we do?"

"You think Mina is in cahoots with the Count?"

"It is a worrying complication, Watson."

"I do not accept it could possibly be the case, my good friend."

"We shall see. Lestrade. What have you to say?"

"For myself, I have worries closer to the present point of our investigation and the whereabouts of the perpetrator. We should examine the method that we will apply in identifying the place in London that Dracula is holding for a base, which we have spoken to earlier. My point being that, if we find that base, then we will halt all of his plans and actions with no further effort." Said Lestrade. "This should be a priority. I have my men interviewing solicitors and land agents regarding any property transactions that have taken place over a period of the last six-months. All leases and purchases of buildings grand enough to satisfy the ego of the monster that we chase."

"What is your geographic area of investigation inspector?"

"We are looking throughout London Sherlock, so as not to restrict the chance of locating the building."

"I think you go too broad, inspector."

"Then, what do you propose, Sherlock?"

"The article in today's Gazette, The Southwark Park Mystery, you recall its contents?"

"Why, yes?"

"Then, Inspector, you would surely have greater fortune focusing on property within a small radius of the Southwark Park area. We know Dracula must have help in his endeavors. There is no other way that he found his way to London. That being the case, I would concentrate on those areas where there have been recent decent into wider criminal activity, unusual behavior, or cruelty to animals. And there you will find the monster's lair. I predict it."

"I will take your advice, Sherlock, and I will move our resources to focus upon that range. But for now, they require my attendance back at Scotland Yard."

Lestrade left us to return to his work, and Mrs. Hudson returned to hers. I prepared the telegram to the Harker's, hoping that Sherlock would be incorrect in his assumption. I thought too kindly of Mina Harker. Night was approaching. A chill raised the hairs on the back of my neck like ears of wheat in the wind. What could these hours bring us?

23

THE WRITTEN NOTE

I could not sleep that night and awoke with the hands of the clock both standing upright. Not a degree past midnight. It must have been that the dogs in the neighborhood were howling and by their sound had disturbed me. The whole of London seemed as if it must be full of dogs, all wailing at once. It was a somewhat remarkable volume of noise that I had not considered before this time, or even that there were so many hounds available to form the choir to do so. A strange, hypnotic bird song, perhaps of a nightingale, accompanied the cacophony. The bird enjoying its part in the orchestra.

Then directly outside my bedroom window came a flapping, sounding like the brushing of branches on the glass panes. I knew very well that there were no trees at that opening, a stricken pigeon without doubt, as my thought attempted to rationalize the sound. There was no alternative. I needed to see the occurrence to settle my thoughts about the matter. I made my way across the room, but as I did, the lamp in the room flickered and dimmed in sporadic spirts. The sparse illumination hiding the location of furniture, so that I hit my knee more than once. A damp wick or a lack of paraffin causing the darkness, I considered.

I avoided the furniture by touch more than sight; stumbling my way across the room, found the window and drew back the curtain to peer outside as, behind me, the space moved between light and dark. The street was dull with the cover of a night mist and free from activity, save for a glimpse of a white streak that lightened in its path to pass between the shadows cast reluctantly onto the pavement by the streetlight opposite.

The movement blurring itself instantly into a dark wisp of vapor, dissipating into the fog and disappearing from sight as I attempted to focus my eyes upon it. At the same moment, the dogs suddenly quietened as one, and the lamp in the room regained its strength and vitality. Returning to bed, I fell back to sleep and did not wake again until morning and they thought that all of it had been but a dream.

I shaved, dressed, and made my way to the lounge, hoping Mrs. Hudson had prepared breakfast, and it relieved me to smell the aroma of a hearty feed. It was still before nine and I expected Sherlock would not be active for another hour. So, it surprised me as he was already at the table, busy examining an envelope and card within. Holding it to the light and twisting the paper between his fingers, as he was prone to do with such objects.

“Good morning, Watson. Later than usual this morning!” He said, without diverting his eyes in my direction.

“Good morning, Sherlock. Earlier than usual this morning! Much earlier, what is the game?” I sat before him and engaged in battle with my breakfast.

“A disturbed sleep. An occurrence that has not hindered me once before today. It is most unusual.”

“I too, slept poorly, having the most concentrated dream. It appeared I was in a part of one of those dammed journals. But what have you there?”

"It is an envelope, containing a note, Watson, addressed to us both. Pushed through the door last night."

"What of it, Holmes, what do you find?"

"The writing on the envelope is familiar, the card inside of the type of paper that we have seen before at the scenes of both Seward's and then at Godalming's murder. It is of the same ink, pen and handwriting, this time the cipher not used, and the note signed."

"Show me Holmes." I took the note and examined it myself, getting the same icy chill I received at the Theatre Royal in Exeter as we witnessed that terrible event. It read:

'My Dear Friends,

I hope my visit did not disturb you tremendously last evening. My impatience may be to blame as I am anxiously expecting to meet you in person. Unlike my previous time here, my visit to London has been a happy and a fulfilling one. I am thoroughly enjoying my stay in your plentiful land.

It is important that you sleep well to-night and for the

next two, to prepare your energies. Once my business is finished with those who have sought it. I hold a place that is thereafter kept for you. Although you may not realize the fact, you will bring yourselves to me. And, when you arrive, you are welcome to my house, and you may enter freely and of your own will.

Do not wait for me, as I wait for you.

DRACULA'

"He was around last night! It is a challenge, a threat, Holmes!"

"But a message that reveals more than is written upon it."

"How, so?"

"It sets the timeline for our investigation. It is now Thursday. He determines he will do his work in the next three days. That takes us to Saturday night before he will strike on Sunday. That being the case, we have those hours in which to safeguard the others, and to find his lair. He also expects us to locate it, but not before then. And therefore, he carries with him a mistake, though. He allows us into his realm wherever that may be."

"Lestrade's men may provide hope then."

At that moment, the rattling of sliding hoofs along the cobbles signaled a carriage as it halted within the gloom of the street below. Sherlock had risen from his chair at the table and was standing between the parted curtains, gazing down from the window into the dull neutral-tinted morning.

Standing on tiptoes and looking over his shoulder, I saw that on the pavement three figures had left the cab. They all made their way to the door of 221B Baker Street. It was Mina, and I presumed Jonathan and the boy Quincey. They were in town at the Great Western Railway Hotel as Sherlock had predicted and had received our telegram.

"Before they enter Watson, be quick. Let us arrange the seating so we can observe them all at the same moment. And be sure not to inform any of them of our endeavors."

Beside the single seat that is normally held for visitors to the apartment, we pulled two chairs from the table and set them on either side of it. Our own seating arrangement maintained. A bookending the seating in front of the newly made fire.

The Harker's entered the room, ushered in by Mrs. Hudson and led by Mina, appearing gaunt and pale and weaker since her last visit. Followed by the boy, Quincey, and then Jonathan. I had not met Jonathan prior to this day. He was a tall, slightly built man with handsome features, his complexion was darker, and his hair was grayer than would be expected of a man of his age. The grace of each adult had been passed to the boy. For there was a striking resemblance to both parents within the child. All three carried the same solemn countenance as they introduced themselves.

"I shall get tea for you all." Said Mrs. Hudson as she left towards the kitchen.

"Good day to you all. Please remove your coats. We have a fierce fire in the hearth. From it you shall be quickly warmed. We have seats for you here." Sherlock directed them to the three chairs lined, as we had placed them, in front of the fire. They sat without a word between them. Mrs. Hudson delivered the tea and departed to her own quarters.

"Jonathan, it is good to meet you, after receiving your correspondence those years ago. I regret that without the journals I could do nothing to assist you then. But now is a very different story."

"It is good to meet you finally, also, Mr. Holmes. A lot has happened in the intervening years. I hope that time has not dulled your reasoning, sir."

"Hopefully not. Let us all take a moment to steady our thoughts before we begin." Sherlock said as he positioned himself in his chair and me in mine.

24

THE VISITOR

Sherlock Holmes sat silently for a few minutes with his fingers pressed tightly together at their tips. His legs stretched out to their full extent in front of him, and his gaze directed upward to the ceiling. Then he took down from the rack close to his right hand, the old and oily clay pipe, which was to him as a counsellor. Having lit it, he leaned back in his chair, with the thick blue cloud-wreaths spinning up from him, and a look of infinite languor in his face. He sat coiled in his armchair, his haggard and ascetic face hardly visible amid the blue swirl of his tobacco smoke, his black brows drawn down, his forehead contracted, his eyes vacant and far away.

Finally, he laid down his pipe and spoke.

“Miss Mina, I think now is the time that you tell all in this room the matter leading to the reason for your original visit to Baker Street.”

“Mr. Holmes I could not have the entire story, though, I knew something was afoot. It was not until I read the papers over the following days, reporting the dreadful happenings to both poor Dr. Seward and Lord Godalming, I had no corroboration of what I was dreaming was the truth.”

“For most part of the previous six years, Jonathan has encountered dreadful night after dreadful night. Hardly sleeping, twisting, muttering, and roaming. I am so glad that he has plenty of work to perform, for such matters keep his mind off the terrible things that he seems to experience at night; and oh, I have rejoiced that he is no longer weighed down with the responsibility of his new position. I knew he would be true to himself, and now how proud I am to see my Jonathan rising to the height of his advancement and keeping pace in all ways with the obligations that come upon him. He takes care of our family, but I fear that is not enough.”

Jonathan sat and gazed with sadness at his wife. His face grew pale and his eyes filled with tears. The boy Quincey remained steady in his focus, staring straight ahead upon the fire and the quivering of its flames, his mind on other things, in particular a loudly ticking silver pocket watch. The watch decorated on its rear with the embossed image of the Greek god Zeuss.

"Jonathan, being the exclusive matter of your concern?"

"I have not told you all of what I am aware, Mr. Holmes."

"It is how I suspected it to be. Please continue. Hide nothing, as all that you say will be important for us to know how we will start the end of this battle."

"I often wondered if there is any truth in it at all. How could I know that the fearful Count could resurrect and was coming to London? It looked to be an impossibility, my imagination being driven by Jonathan's restless sleeping, full of words and visions, until that night a month ago."

"We were both sleeping, and something awoke me being present in the room. I turned to wake Jonathan, but found that he slept so soundly that it seemed as if it was he who had taken the sleeping draught, and not I. I tried, but I could not wake him. This caused me a great fear, and I looked around, terrified. Then indeed, my heart sank within me: beside the bed, as if he had stepped out of the mist, or rather as if the mist had turned into his figure, was the Count."

Jonathan was still and quiet; but over his face, as the awful narrative went on, came a grey look which deepened and deepened in the morning light. He stood suddenly. "You did not mention that he had visited you!" He grasped Mina's hand before sinking to his knees in front of her. His face plunged into the folds of her dress, and he sobbed. "If he is returned, then all of us are doomed. He will not stop until we are all with him. Quincey too." Mina lifted Jonathan's head and pulled his hand to guide him back to his seat, where he slumped, head in hands.

"I did not need to distress you any more than you are already. That is why I visited with Mr. Sherlock Holmes. He is to assist us. He will help us. That is right, is it not Mr. Holmes?"

"Of course, my dear Mina, but to continue, I need to be certain that I know all the facts. Tell me all between the time of his first visit and now."

"After that night when he appeared I took to issuing the white flowers and powder of the plant around the openings of the house. After that there were no more visitations to me in the home, but he appeared in my dreams and spoke to me often. Calling for me, telling me to come to London."

"What were those messages?"

"He told me in images and words that he was amongst the teeming thousands of London and would seek all that had moved against him. The preparations that he has made are fuller and more general than those he made on his first visit. He has many helpers and a place that sits in the town's heart. There will be no stopping him. I fear his darkness, Mr. Holmes. He repeated many times, that we would all pay dearly."

Jonathan sat back upright. His complexion was paler than when he first arrived, and the rims around his eyes reddened from the tears. He drew a breath and spoke:

"As you know, seven years ago, we all went through the flames; and the happiness of some of us since then is well worth the pain we endured. In the summer of this year, we made a journey to Transylvania, and went over the old ground which was, and is, to us so full of vivid and terrible memories. I can not believe that the things which we had seen with our own eyes and heard with our own ears were living truths. When we got home, we were talking of the old time, which we could all look back on without despair. We could hardly ask anyone, even did we wish to, to accept so wild a story."

"Except we have them now and have little doubt in their content."

"Mr. Holmes, I am of the belief that the Count may have followed us back somehow, from that visit."

"That is a possibility Mr. Harker, but that is yet to be proven. We shall continue to search for the truth because without it we will not endure. I suggest you all return to the hotel and we will take to inform you of our progress as we might make it. You know of the precautions that you need to take."

"Thank you both. We will retire to our hotel knowing that you are on the case and confident that we have not been abandoned in our fight."

The Harker's thanked us more than once during their exit. I hoped they would be safe, but I had seen the monster in action and feared for all of their safety. Quincey had not spoken until his departure; he had a remarkable look of defiance upon his face as he left the apartment. It was then that I approached Sherlock regarding his significant omission.

"You did not inform them that Van Helsing arrives tomorrow, Holmes."

"I fear Dracula has a direct line to the thoughts and dreams of Mrs. Harker. And he knows whatever she sees or hears. We will need to use that channel to our advantage in the impending days."

25

THE MURDERED PASSENGER

Sherlock once told me that "No man burdens his mind with unimportant matters unless he has some excellent reason."

I discovered early in our acquaintance that his ignorance was as remarkable as his knowledge. Of contemporary literature, philosophy, and politics, he appeared to know next to nothing. Nor even of the composition of the Solar System. That any civilized human being in this nineteenth century should not be aware that the earth travelled round the sun appeared to be to me such an extraordinary fact that I could hardly realize it.

“You appear to be astonished,” he said, smiling at my expression of surprise. “Now that I know it, I shall do my best to forget it.”

“To forget it!”

“You should note.” He explained, “I consider that a man’s brain at its beginning is like a little empty attic, and you have to stock it with such furniture as you choose. A fool takes in all the lumber of every sort that he comes across, so that the knowledge which might be useful to him gets crowded out. Jumbled up with a lot of other things so that he has a difficulty in laying his hands upon it. Now the skillful workman is very careful indeed what he takes into his brain-attic. He will have nothing but the tools which may help him in doing his work, but of these he has a large assortment, and all in the most perfect order. It is a mistake to think that little room has elastic walls and can distend to any extent. Depend upon it, there comes a time when, for every addition of knowledge, you forget something that you knew before. It is of the highest importance, therefore, not to have useless facts elbowing out the useful ones.”

"But the Solar System!" I protested.

"What the deuce is it to me?" he interrupted impatiently; "you say that we go round the sun. If we went round the moon, it would not make a pennyworth of difference to me or to my work."

And that, my reader, is why the man is a genius.

"Watson, we must spend this afternoon wisely. Out of the purview of Mina, as we must keep her ignorant of our intent so she cannot tell what she knows not, and before Van Helsing arrives, we need to gather the daily newspapers and examine them for unusual or exaggerated events. Any happening where we cannot reason the explanation easily."

On our ask, Mrs. Hudson departed to a news vendor close to the apartment and returned with several of the day's newspapers. Most of the articles were of a non-local occurrence, including the unfortunate missives of Prime Minister Rosebery, great floods in parts of the country, discrepancies of accounting at the Royal Mint and the progression of certain discoveries in science. The local news was full of mundane articles of petty theft, building fires, runaway carts. Nothing stood out until...

“Here, Sherlock, I have one in the Gazette. THE MURDERED PASSENGER. Last night, in the shadow of St. Olave’s Union Workhouse, on Tanner Street in Bermondsey, there occurred a most peculiar event. An empty passenger cab was passing along the same street. Without warning, the driver was met by a man who hailed him down and jumped hastily in the coach before the cab had come to a halt. The passenger ordered the driver to proceed at speed. The driver lashed into his horse, and the vehicle plunged forward and headed onto Bermondsey Street. When the cab came to a halt beside the Church of Mary Magdalene, the passenger was lying on his seat with his head rolling upon his shoulder, with his throat pierced. A long stream of loose blood trickled slowly down from his neck over his clothes. They took the cabby in a distraught humor into custody and there he remains while they investigate further the case.”

“We need to speak to the cabby today; contact Lestrade and get us access to question the man before they release him.”

Within the hour we met Lestrade at the Police Station on Bermondsey Street, where the cabby is being held. Sherlock, Lestrade and I sat in a small room in front of a small table. Behind and hunched over it sat a shivering small man in his fifties. The hair on his head lank and thin, exposing the scalp beneath. He looked up at us, his face unshaven and his eyes wide, flittering between us and the barred window behind.

"I have done nothing here; I know not what caused that man to lose his life. They will take me for a murderer, you must hear me. This is the truth." The man said in quick fashion before we had any opportunity of introducing ourselves.

"My good man. I am Sherlock Holmes, this is Inspector Lestrade and my good friend Dr. Watson. We are not here because we think you are a murderer. But others may. Tell us exactly what happened that night. Starting at the beginning, a saving no part of the events. First your name, sir?"

"I am Walter Padbury."

"Now, Walter, tell us all you know."

In a gravelly voice, seemingly hoarse with terror that he had experienced, Walter told his story. "I was ending the night, having plenty of business before this happened. It had been an evening that brought with it a heavy fog. A strange mist that clung to the street and prevented sight of objects greater than thirty paces distant. The gloom had delivered many passengers to my cab, as they wanted to secure a safe way to home.

The fog thickened as the night progressed, so much so I determined it was becoming unsafe to drive. I should not have stopped, and tried not to, but the man ran the carriage down and was in the cab before the wheels had halted. I asked him where he would be going. 'Drive for your life!' the man shouted. 'Drive like the devil! For he is on my tail. I have got many gold sovereigns. You shall have whatever you ask.' I had only driven a few steps when the passenger shouted, 'Go left! For heaven's sake, left! Do not you hear them: They'll catch us, you fool, go on, I tell you!' Only moments later, the passenger cried out again. 'They are behind us!' I looked around; I saw only the confines of the fog, which was now churning in a whirlpool. The man was leaning out of the side of the cab; I noticed his face was ghastly white, his eyes seemingly frantic with terror, and his hands clutched fearfully at the casement the window."

"Was there anything behind?"

"No. when I looked the road was full of a swirling fog, both behind and in front with not a soul in sight. It was then I felt my blood run cold. This man, was he a madman, or even something worse."

"Something worse?"

"You know. The stories of the doctor man seen around these parts, attacking children. In the park."

"Yes, we have seen such reports. He was not the man though, so please continue."

"No, he was not the man. It was now close to midnight. The streets were empty of people, the fog holding any issue of sound within it. It was too silent. There was only the repeat from the shoes of my horse. I strained my ears to listen, to catch any sound that might come from the distance, but I could hear nothing. But then, moments later, I fancied that there was the faint sound borne on the breeze, like the flapping of great wings. I thought it may be a night-owl. I looked round expectantly to see it or the like. But I still found that the view to the rear was empty, nothing but the yellow grey of the fog. Even the light of the streetlamps was extinguished. Suddenly, the strange terror built within me and seized at my heart at the same time as I felt the waft of wings close to my face. The force of it took my cap off, and I stopped the cab to set down to retrieve it. I descended hastily from my box onto the street. I still saw nothing in the quickly thickening fog, the color of which got a deeper brown. Then, having recovered my cap, I returned to the cab and lifted myself to the window. Calling out to the passenger; but there was no answer. It was then that I opened the door, and the horror came upon me. Once I saw the scene, I fell back onto the street."

"What did you observe?"

"The man was upright but crumpled, his head twisted backwards with the throat exposed. The shirt pulled back, and the collar torn. His face, from what I recall, was ghastly white and the eyes wide open and set upon the roof of the cab."

"What about the injuries?"

"The throat untorn, but two small punctures existed here." Walter pointed to his neck and to the region of the jugular, jabbing at it with two fingers, "Here, right here. The blood still trickling down the man's clothing."

"You saw no other?"

"No, there was no one. All I know is that I did not do this thing! You must believe me!"

"I am certain this murder did not involve you, and Inspector Lestrade here will help you get out of here. But one last thing. Where did your passenger appear from, do you suppose?"

"The workhouse on Tanner Street. St. Olave's Union Workhouse. The building that I was passing by when the man appeared. There could be no other place. I could smell it on his clothing."

26

THE WORKHOUSE

We left the police station behind us, stepping into the light of the street filtered by the smoke and haze of industrial activity. Lestrade was working to release the poor cabby from custody. We knew Walter Padbury had no part in the man's murder.

During the interview Lestrade had handed Sherlock a scrap of paper, which contained a name but nothing more. They also found a single gold coin on the body, freshly minted, not a scratch upon it, with Queen Victoria on the face and an illustration of St. George fighting the

Dragon on its reverse. Lestrade kept the coin close at hand, holding the gleaming metal between his thumb and forefinger in a flamboyant display towards Sherlock's examination. Sherlock nodded, and Lestrade replaced it into a cotton handkerchief and then into his pocket. We continued towards St. Olave's workhouse.

The workhouse was close-by the police station, a distance of less than ten minutes of walking time along Bermondsey Street. The facility, designed with purpose to help the throngs of the poor and unfortunate souls who found themselves set on hard times. It is not a place for those who did not need to be there by choice. The brick building stood four stories high, the façade stained by the steady growth of moss and the filthy industry of the area. Tanners' yards, skinners, and trades that partook in the raw and base profession of the leather processing business.

As we grew closer to our destination so the stink in the air grew stronger. A stench delivered by the activities in the area. Added to by the dire lack of cleanliness in and around the building. This part of the city was not one that would attract respectable citizens. The air effectively poisoned by the squalor we should soon discover for ourselves.

I knew of the place, having read a recent report in the Lancet medical journal, which in the words of the document stated that the accommodation was 'not fit for a dog'. Arrangements made were 'altogether brutal'. Beds were 'long boxes used previously to carry oranges or grapefruit, with a wooden log for a pillow.' According to the report, the Guardians of Bermondsey were unique 'in their mode of lodging the homeless poor'.

"A perfect lair for the Count, then Sherlock?" I postulated.

"Let us discover that only through the evidence we find, Watson."

The door to the front entrance locked, being guarded from unauthorized access. Barred to deter those desperate for accommodation, who often tried to storm the door. Sherlock hammered his fist against it. The door soon opened and a man in his thirties answered. He did not look directly at our faces, but immediately at our feet. Then without further glance, said, "can I help you gentleman? You are obviously not here for a place."

"Yes, you may. We call in order to visit with the Master of the establishment." Sherlock said.

"That will be Mr. Parkinson. You may follow me. Please, watch your step for there may be items you do not want to catch to your shoes, them being so shiny and nicely fitting like. You can remove them if you prefer." The guard pointed to a stack of miscellaneous shoes and boots stacked close to the doorway. He closed the door and locked it behind us. Placing the key amongst many others hanging together beside the door.

Having kept our footwear, we introduced ourselves. The man said no more, but escorted us, leading a path through a maze of winding corridors. Introducing on both sides of the path, rooms filled with noise, odor, and activity. In most of the dimly lit spaces I observed inmates.

I shall call them such, even though they were free to leave. They were all men, and all wore the same uniform of a gray coat and waistcoats of cloth with red collar, white metal buttons, olive corduroy trousers, cotton shirts, ill-fitting strong shoes, and coarse hats. There were no women present as the accommodation set in place a rigorous segregation. The men were engaged to work in oakum picking, the unravelling of coarse rope into strands for re-use. A thankless repetitive task, which took a heavy price on the skin of their hands and fingers.

Those new to it suffered with raw and blistered flesh through the abrasive nature of the material.

Eventually we arrived at the Master's office, having the door marked such. The porter knocked, entered, and introduced us. "I have Mr. Sherlock Holmes and his companion to visit with you, Sir". The Master did not show any movement of life and remained seated behind a large oak desk. Finely polished and holding many accessories. A brass desk lamp, a gold-ivory handled letter opener and fine leather writing pad all did not keep well with the environment that we had journeyed through.

"Mr. Holmes. I believe that I have heard of you, the famous detective! This is a pleasure Mr. Holmes, let me introduce myself. I am William Parkinson, the Master of St. Olave's. This is my wife, Ann. What brings you both to our establishment?"

"Certainly not the air, my good fellow! We come seeking information regarding a deadly errand. There was a murder last night. A passing cab picked the victim up outside this address last evening." Sherlock took the scrap of paper that Lestrade had given him from his pocket. "The papers found on the body of the dead man identified him as Bill Guy. Do you have anyone of that name here?"

"Well, we have over two hundred and sixty inmates. They are all listed in our records. If he was here, then the ledger will tell." Parkinson responded in a broad northern English accent. He was a stout man in his forties, well dressed and well fed, in contrast to those in his keeping. His wife, Ann, the Matron and several years younger, passed him the bound leather ledger held between others from the bookshelf behind her. Parkinson opened the thick journal, each leaf carrying dozens of names, and moved to the page. Parkinson ran his index finger down the list and stopped midway along.

"Here. Yes, Guy... William. He is here. He was the murdered man? What happened to him?"

"Yes, that was he. We are still investigating Mr. Parkinson. Did you not miss him today?"

"It has not been reported to me yet, but they marked him in the ledger as being in the infirmary for two days. We can visit with the nurse on duty to establish the facts."

We headed to the infirmary. Passing through the sweet stench that filled the corridors and hung onto your clothing like cobwebs. Once there, we found a long room lined with the boxes used as beds. Each occupied with a twisted but motionless body of a man, except for one. It was striking that even in the dim light the faces all stared at the ceiling and shone with a deathly whiteness to them. A pallor that we had seen before but in not so many at the same moment. A dull, sullen, woe-begone look. Jane Freeman was the nurse on duty that day. Parkinson approached her.

"Nurse Freeman. Bill Guy is murdered it seems. Did he leave here, did you see him at any part of last night?" Asked Parkinson.

"Murdered! No! But that is his bed. It was empty when I started the day at six this morning. We summarized he had gone on his own way and changed the bed linen. We will fill it with another in minutes. There are many wanting a bed. Nurse Maroney mentioned nothing when we exchanged shifts this morning. However, she looked tired and her complexion shallow."

"You suspected nothing fowl, Nurse Freeman?" Asked Sherlock.

"No, although he was perhaps livelier than the others that we see here. Although we found some disturbing things hidden within the bed and its slats."

"What things, Nurse Freeman?"

"Remnants of half-eaten rodents. All dry and exhausted of their blood, as though something had sucked them dry. The man was surely insane."

"The man Guy and his symptoms differed greatly from the others stored here?"

"They admitted him to bed two nights since. He had nervous utterings and a fear about him, of far greater intensity than the others."

"For what subjects did he speak of?"

"He was mostly incoherent. I do recall, he had said as he sat on the edge of the bed. 'I am here to do your bidding, master. I am your slave, and you will reward me, for I shall be faithful. I will be faithful now that you are near. You will not pass me by, will you, dear master, in your distribution of good things?' I can only think he was talking about Mr. Parkinson, the Master before you."

"Yes, the men all have great respect for me, Mr. Holmes." Said Parkinson, blowing his chest out like the plumage of a proud peacock.

"I fear that there may be another, Sir. One that visits this establishment and takes his fill."

"I do not understand, Mr. Holmes."

"I do not wonder, sir! The patients here, they all suffer with the same malady?" Asked Sherlock.

"It seems to be the case. They arrive with a degree of paranoia, which then settles into a melancholy countenance. They soon fade but are soon replaced with another to fill their bed. We have no answer to their illness." Said the Nurse.

Sherlock examined the waste container next to the nurse's station, moved to examine one patient. Then another three, looking closely at the area of their necks and then approaching closer, his nose in proximity to their face to take in their breath. He then examined the now empty bed previously occupied by the murdered man. He ran his fingers between the headboard and the meagre padding of the mattress, then shifted the sole of his right boot upon the floor close to the side of the bed.

"I see. Now I see. We need to return to Baker Street Watson and pull this riddle together."

We left the confines of the hell that was the workhouse. I hoped never to return to such a place. It is all as described by Dickens in his fictional novels but brought to life in such fabulous and horrendous detail.

27

FEEDING FRENZY

I write this account with the benefit of knowledge discovered only at a time after the finalization of this case, but certainly within the mind of Sherlock, well beforehand.

Mary Maroney was the youngest of the nursing staff at the workhouse. She was twenty-nine and had an underlying timid disposition, albeit now hardened somewhat by her eight years at the workhouse. Mary was small in stature, perhaps less than five feet. Her normally rosy complexion was dimmer than usual, and her auburn hair tucked under the starched white hat showed a hint of gray at its roots. She had not noticed.

Tonight, a heavy and foreboding atmosphere hung over and within the workhouse infirmary. It unsettled the duty nurse. Her clothes felt heavy. The goosebumps kept appearing on her arms without cause. She did not consider the issue as she had a tiredness overwhelming her. Something had happened the previous night, but she could not fully recall the events. Mary had no inkling that this evening would see the murder of Bill Guy.

Through her years of experience, Mary had handled patients with illnesses prevalent in such institutions. Measles, eye infections, smallpox, dysentery, scarlet and typhus fevers, and cholera, amongst the most common. She was familiar with them all. This present disease was spreading through the institution without cause.

The doctor who had visited last had prescribed citrus fruit to the patients, hoping their malady was not the beginning of the scurvy. The symptoms were very different. They seemed to be more psychological, with all the patients deteriorating at the same pace. Placid during the day and increasingly disturbed during the night. Her hand held the side of her neck and rubbed it back and forth as she recalled a strange dreamlike encounter the previous night. She was tired.

Mary noted, many if not all the patients, although languid until the end of the day, had become beset with greater unease as the night grew darker and even more so towards midnight. The murmurings of the patients becoming a chorus of seemingly unordered words, delivered with no apparent direction. The listener, however, would discover the commonalities of the vocabulary being the most disturbing aspect of the condition. All calling in a garbled tongue for the master. She would only calm the twisting, moaning bodies with the administration of a dose of strong opiate medicine, which took effect with some rapidity.

This evening, Mary had started her shift at five o'clock and was expecting the progression of those in her care to deteriorate, as it had the previous nights. There were twenty-six beds on the ward, thirteen on each side of the infirmary room. Her desk sat at the far end. All the beds occupied, the men in them became increasingly disturbed.

All except Bill Guy, accommodated at the end of the row closest to the entrance door and furthest distance from the nurse's desk. Mary prepared doses of laudanum. Setting each in a small paper cup, readying herself to administer the opiate to all in her care. As darkness threw its cloak over the world outside, dogs in the neighborhood wailed. Mary walked along the line of beds towards the entrance door. She looked towards Bill's bed and found him in the opposite humor to the others, sitting, seemingly as contented as he could be. As she grew closer, she noticed there were flies all around him. Suddenly his hands darted back and forth with the rapidity of a mongoose fighting a snake. Catching the flies in his fingers, pushing them towards his lips before eating them. Squashing them like grapes between his teeth. He was keeping note of his capture by making nail-marks on the edge of the wooden crate bed frame, in the gap between what acted as the headboard and the padding that put itself as a mattress.

When Mary got closer, Bill turned to look at her directly with a stare and awkward smile, folding his arms tightly to hold them against involuntary movement. He apologized for his bad conduct, and asked in a very humble, cringing way to be exempted from the calming dose.

Mary thought it well to humor him, but when looking at the floor she noted there were peelings from the grapefruit spread about, Bill was reaping quite a harvest from the flies settling upon it. He turned from eating them to putting them into a small container. For a moment or two he looked very sad, and said in a sort of far-away voice, as though saying it rather to himself than to Mary:

"All over! All over! He has deserted me. No hope for me now unless I do it for myself!" Then suddenly turning to Mary resolutely, he said: "Nurse, won't you be very good to me and let me have a little more fruit? I think it would be good for me."

"And the flies?" She inquired.

"Yes! The flies like it, too, and I like the flies; therefore, I like it." Mary bought him a new fruit, and left him as happy a man, she supposed, as any in the world.

Mary stood for a moment and peered through the upper barred window of the infirmary at the sunset. A wonderful smoky beauty over London, with its lurid light and inky shadows and all the marvelous tints brought into vision on foul clouds and atop the river fog. A heavy contrast with the grim, colorless interior of the cold workhouse institution. Through the low hanging translucent mist, the red disc dropped below the horizon and the night began. As it sank, Bill Guy sang out.

"The blood is the life! The blood is the life!"

At that moment, many of the patients gyrating within their beds moaned and wailed. As in time and rhythm with each other. Mary ran to the station to secure the calming tincture for administration to those in her care. As her back turned, Bill grabbed his jacket off the hook next to his bed and made steps out of the entrance door of the infirmary into the dark corridor that would lead him to freedom.

The far end of the corridor made a bright rectangle, the light at the main door. The porter was not there. Bill stepped towards his escape. The distance to the exit became clouded with a vapor, a mist, which took a familiar form. He knew what, and who, that was, and did not want to meet him this evening. Bill increased his pace. Before he arrived at the door of his escape, ahead of him, the form materialized. It was not alone; two others flanked it. A swirling fog extruding arms, legs, torsos, and heads.

The figure in front was Dracula, his face was a very strong

aquiline, with a high bridge of the thin nose and peculiarly arched nostrils; with lofty domed forehead and hair growing scantily round the temples, but profusely elsewhere. His eyebrows were very massive, almost meeting over the nose, with bushy hair that seemed to curl in its own profusion. The mouth fixed and rather cruel looking, with peculiarly sharp white teeth protruding over the lips, whose remarkable ruddiness showed astonishing vitality in a man of his years. For the rest, his ears were pale, and at the tops extremely pointed. The chin was broad and strong, and the cheeks firm though thin. The general effect was one of extraordinary pallor. Billy stepped away, creating a greater distance between them.

"Master, they are ready for you. Well prepared to supply you with all that you need. Your friends too."

"But where do you head to? Do you try to go, to run, do you fear for life? Do not have such concerns? There is no reason, for you are free to go. Have I not paid you in gold for your services? You are no longer required to stay here. Go my man, return to your home, wherever that may be."

The Count and his two accomplices stood to one side and allowed Bill to pass. He felt their breath on the back of his neck as he moved toward the exit. He was barefoot. The door secured and would need a key. Having no shoes, he dove into the pile stacked against the entrance wall. He located a pair of his size and threw them on, their laces untied. Bill's fingers grasped at the set of keys hanging beside the door. It took him four tries before he found the correct fit. It turned in its hole and the door opened. Bill hurried out. He had escaped and now would need to travel away from this place as quickly as possible. He heard the cab approaching long before it appeared before him out of the mist like a ghost ship. The three vampires had moved into the infirmary and were taking their fill. Dancing from bed to bed, draining each dormant patient of a portion of their lifeblood.

Dracula, the first through the door to the ward, had rushed forward, taken hold of the nurse and bent her backwards to look in her eyes. He paused, and she could hear the churning sound of his tongue as it licked his teeth and lips and could feel the fiery breath on her neck.

Then the skin of her throat tingled as one's flesh does when the hand that is to tickle it approaches nearer, nearer. She could feel the soft, shivering touch of the lips on the supersensitive skin of her throat, and the hard dents of two sharp teeth, just touching and pausing there. Then Dracula pushed through the skin and into the vein, quickly taking his fill. The nurse fainting as he withdrew the blood in large flowing gulps. The warm liquid spilling down the side of his mouth, over his chin and down his neck.

It was only a matter of minutes until the workhouse door slammed with the exit of Bill onto the Street. The Count threw the nurse down. She would recover by daybreak and recall little of the event. Dracula then looked over his shoulder. His flaming red eyes widened as he hurried to the door. The others continued their feeding frenzy, being now almost halfway down each row of beds.

“Feed on my good fellows, feed on. Take care to leave your donors away from death. We can return to replenish when the need takes us. Then meet me at the lair as I have business to resolve before I return.”

As Dracula departed St. Olave’s, he gazed upon the rear of the carriage as it sped away. Swallowed by the fog, it disappeared. The quiet broken by hooves clattering upon the cobbled street. His form shifted from solid to vapor back to solid. Now a giant bat, unfolding great wings of leather, to lift him into the blanket of dense fog, summoned on his command. There would be no escape for his prey.

He flew after the cab, catching it within three full, almost silent beats of his wings. Bill hung out the window, terrified, turning to shout instructions at the driver. His gaze met Dracula's piercing red eyes fully, and he knew it was the end. The Count flew to a close pass of the cab, grazing the driver's head and displacing the cap from it into the street.

The cabby stopped the vehicle and spent twenty paces to retrieve his hat. In the same moment that he did so, Dracula reformed and entered the cabin from the opposite side. Billy gasped but could not release a cry of any value. His throat dry with fear, knowing that this was the end.

"Yes, I have done with your services, but not with your lifeblood. I shall take that now, together with the gold pieces left in your pocket!" Dracula growled in a low grumbling voice, an octave below a man's normal speech. In one movement he settled on Bill's neck, draining the man of what remained of his life.

His clawed fingers explored the pocket of his victim, removing all but one sovereign previously given as payment. There was no struggle, only a few nervous twitches of the fingers and left leg. A loose shoe fell from the jerking foot to the floor of the carriage. The task done.

28

INSPIRATION AND TELEGRAM

We left the workhouse, exiting its inhumane walls and ghastly stench, and hailed the first cab that we came across. The discussion of our findings will take place on our return to the comfort of Baker Street. When we arrived, the fire was blazing in the hearth; the air was fresher than the stench of London air that hung outside, and Mrs. Hudson had served tea and sandwiches.

Sherlock slumped into his chair and took again to his

pipe, the smoke of it adding to the haze of the dim evening light entering the room. If it were not for the putrid air and smog that filled the street, I would have opened the window to disperse the cloud. It had been the strangest of days, and I was eager to find out more of Sherlock's contemplations.

"My thoughts of the peculiar nature of the story make me eager to have every detail at my disposal. When I have determined some slight sign of the course of events, I can guide myself by the thousands of other comparable cases which occur to my memory. In the present instance I am forced to admit that the facts are, to the best of my belief, extraordinary. I am therefore, to build the solution from the parts that we have in our hands."

"What think you of the workhouse and that wretched fellow Guy?"

"I suspect the victim in this case was working hand in hand with Dracula. Bill Guy was providing access to the workhouse. The Count, for some obscure reason, requires permission, given by free will, to enter the premises."

"How do you deduce that from the evidence we have Holmes?"

"What evidence do you say we have, my dear friend?"

"Well, we have the cabby who took the fateful passenger to his death. We have the workhouse, full of men with certain similar maladies that appear in line to what we have read in the journals and seen with our own eyes. The behavior of the victim appearing odd, again similar to that observed by Dr. Seward in his writings. All having the symptoms of the disease of contact with Dracula."

"And, what more, Watson?"

"Well, it is all, is it not?"

"Well, now, in considering this case, there are several observations that you miss. What of the use of the opiate to calm all the patients, all except the victim? The marks on all the necks of those in the infirmary, the sugar on the infirmary floor, the marks on the bedframe, and of the night nurse having an illness."

"That all directs only to Dracula! I may have misplaced some of what you mention, but the conclusion remains the same, does it not?"

"No, you are too quick in your conjecture, Watson. There was citrus peel on the floor, close to the bed of the victim. This was probably used to attract insects, creatures that would be nothing more than snacks to the man, taking the meager portion of blood to sustain his energy. As he had from the rats drained and hidden in his bed. The marks upon the bedframe, some form of measure I propose, scratched with the fingernails."

"The nurse did not provide him with laudanum as she did with the other patients. One cup remained at the nurse's desk. I would say that this was because he was exhibiting a calmness not observed in the other patients. The escape already planned. I inspected the men within each row of beds. All had bite patterns."

"At each throat those marks having a certain uniqueness to them. The marks were similarly different. The gap between the canines used to puncture the skin and draw from the jugular, being narrower than those that we know to belong to Dracula. These differences are then coming from the jaws and teeth of two individuals, perhaps not yet known to us."

"There are others? More of these beasts?" I asked.

"Yes, companions to Dracula. At least two, for now."

"They are multiplying!"

"More unnerving, Watson, as the infected do not quite die,

living between the worlds, so they resurrect and seek the same lifeblood that the Count takes at his leisure. A virus will breed and mutate in its host. The monsters pass on their curse as they take their fill. The whole of nighttime London will soon be in danger if it is not already so."

"We need to find them, Holmes! Where are we to look, where are they hiding? The journals say that they will need to retire during daylight hours."

"I am narrowing the location, Watson. Let us consider the most recent incidents and their geography. The assaults in Southwark Park, St. Olave's workhouse, Bermondsey Street and the Royal Mint."

"The Royal Mint?"

"Yes, Watson. The Royal Mint, north of the river and close to the St. Katherine Docks. The place that they refine and store gold coins. Lestrade showed us the brand-new gold sovereign as found on the victim, marked with this year, 1894. Now, if we draw a radius that envelops those landmarks, we should surely locate the lair, being situated to find easy access to these points."

"But still Holmes, how do you see that connection."

"Elementary, my dear Watson. You recall your reading of the newspaper articles prior to the discovery of the one pertaining to the 'Murdered Passenger'? Remarking on an article that discussed an accounting error at the Royal Mint. I placed that information into my mind, over the important issue of the composition of the Solar System! An accounting error or theft. The one and the same I propose. We know Dracula covets gold second only to blood. There is the connection."

"Remarkable, Holmes!"

At that moment there was a knock at the front door off Baker Street. Mrs. Hudson appeared shortly afterwards, climbing the stairs with telegram in hand.

"Becoming a right postal office, it is. I shall be glad when it has calmed again. These stairs are steep and many." Said Mrs. Hudson, passing the envelope to Sherlock.

"Thank you, Mrs. Hudson."

Sherlock opened the envelope. It was a communication from Van Helsing; he read aloud:

"Telegram: Sherlock Holmes, 221B Baker Street London England. Arrive at Paddington 10:14 tomorrow. Please meet there. Tell no-one. Professor Van Helsing."

"So, he arrives tomorrow. Not a word of this to anyone, including Lestrade, who we must inform of our findings. The police need to concentrate on a smaller area of buildings. There are many wharves, mills, docks, and other dark buildings that will require investigation. I suspect the lair to be positioned between the Great Eastern railroad to the north and the South Eastern railroad to the south."

"I shall get word to Lestrade. We should meet with him after our contact with Van Helsing. We need to draw a net round this man from which he cannot escape."

"Yes, also let us, without delay, send Mrs. Hudson to the market before it ends. There, she may secure some garlic cloves as our protection tonight. Dracula has revealed to us he knows our lodgings and we must heed the guidance and remedies of Van Helsing."

Mrs. Hudson was successful in her quest and taken aback when Sherlock took the cloves from her and draped one in each window and above each entrance to the house.

29

THE PROFESSOR ARRIVES

Friday morning started into another clear, although hazy, London sky. The frost was keen, and the defense of the apartment had held, with no sign of intrusion or any attempt thereof. I had enjoyed a good night's sleep, hearing no sounds since I had remained undisturbed. I woke as fresh as a lark at eight and readied myself for the day. Unusually for his habit, Sherlock was already at the table and as we partook of Mrs. Hudson's finest breakfast, his countenance showed that he had rested well himself.

A good sign that his thoughts on the matter were coalescing towards a solution.

"This morning we have urgent business, Watson. The day will be the turning point in this investigation. I predict it."

"I jolly well hope so Holmes, we are seemingly always running behind the villain, sometime by greater than a step."

"He is leaving a marked trail, my good man. Breadcrumbs that will lead us to his demise. First, we must collect Van Helsing from Paddington Station."

"Do you warrant that the Harker's will be in good stead at the hotel?"

"We will visit with them this evening, after I have discussed the matter with Van Helsing."

Our cab made good time to the station, and we waited in proximity to the platform for the train. It had crossed my mind. Surely Dracula will have our movements closely watched. He will certainly have helpers in his employ to act as his eyes, even in the daylight. I glanced furtively around the station, picking out strangers either seated, paused, or going about their business. Anyone of these men, women or children could be the reporters of our actions.

“What on earth are you about now, Watson?”

“I am canvassing the area to see if there are any eyes upon us.”

“Any man observing your current behavior will certainly have theirs upon you, Watson, and that is part of our game. We must allow our adversary to claim knowledge of the events that are now transpiring. It matters more to him of what we do than it does to us. Within all of this we will take our own path.”

“I am sure that you now have me confused Holmes.”

“Keep up with your observations, Watson, that is the way.”

At that moment, the heavy rumble, vibration, and high-pitched hissing of expressed steam heralded the ten fourteen and with it, Professor Van Helsing. After a few minutes, passengers appeared through the gates into the arrival area. We monitored the platform as each passenger emerged, noting the appearance of each against our own construction of the Professor’s appearance. Even though neither of us have ever met him before.

Then a man strode towards us. He was of medium height, strongly built, with his shoulders set back over a broad chest and a neck well balanced on the trunk as the head is on the neck. His head, striking one at once as indicative of thought and power. Being noble, well-sized, broad, and large behind the ears.

A clean-shaven face, showing a hard, square chin, a large resolute, mobile mouth, a good-sized nose, rather straight, but with quick, sensitive nostrils, that seem to broaden as the big bushy brows come down and the mouth straightens. The forehead, broad and fine, rising at first almost straight and then sloping back above two bumps or ridges wide apart, such a forehead that the reddish hair cannot possibly tumble over it, but fall naturally back and to the sides. The big, dark blue eyes set wide apart.

"That is the man Watson, help him with his luggage to our cab."

"You are certain Sherlock?"

"View his left leg Watson, the trouser held tight with a bicycle tie, and the jacket stretched at the shoulders but not yet worn at the elbows. Do not folks of only a certain status in Amsterdam get along by means of the bicycle, a professor being one?"

"Professor?" I asked as I approached the man.

"Yes, that is me." Van Helsing replied, his accent betraying his identity.

"Let me take your bags. I am Dr. Watson, and this is my companion Sherlock Holmes."

"Thank you, this is very good to be here, and better to be meeting now you both. I would wish to be on the better circumstance though. Very unfortunate. Have you informed Ms. Mina yet?"

"No, we will do so after we discuss the situation Professor, first we will return to Baker Street and get you accommodated."

"That is the best. We must become without compassion or hope in this matter. I will explain it when we return to your home."

Professor Van Helsing is a seemingly arbitrary man; this

is because he knows what he is talking about better than anyone else. From what we have found in all the journals is that he is a philosopher and a metaphysician, and one of the most advanced scientists of his day, and he has an absolutely open mind. This, with an iron nerve, a temper of that will not break easily, and indomitable resolution, self-command, and toleration exalted from virtues to blessings, and the kindliest and truest heart that beats, these form his equipment for the noble work he is doing for humanity, work both in theory and practice, for his views are as wide as his all-embracing sympathy.

We arrived back at 221B, Mrs. Hudson had prepared a room and the Professor refreshed himself before joining Sherlock and I in the study. Sherlock, seated in his usual chair and I in mine, contemplated the moment. Van Helsing took to the remaining chair, set as it normally would be between us and facing the warmth of the fire.

Sherlock spoke for a good twenty minutes about the case and what we have observed. He relayed his thought. The murders of Dr. Seward and Godalming were certainly part of a sequence of vengeance, which in his mind was not yet complete. One conclusion he brought to light was that the proximity of all the incidents led to the lair being within a certain radius. The Harker's and Van Helsing himself were most probably on the list, but their order not yet discovered.

Sherlock, as was his habit, stretched out into his longest form and centered his fingers on one another. He pulled his knees upward and sat forward.

"Professor, what do you know of all this, how should we progress?"

30

THE VAMPIRE

The room fell silent for a moment save the steady tick of the clock on the mantle; a sound driven by the rhythmical swing of its pendulum. The hands of time showed eleven twenty-three. The fire below flickered; its flames leapt to kiss the back of the blackened hearth. Van Helsing, his blue eyes glistening, said solemnly.

“You have seen it yourselves. Even if it is hard to know, there are such beings as vampires. Even had we not the proof. The teachings and the records of the past give account enough for sane people. Although, at the first I too was sceptic."

"The nosferatu do not die like the bee when he stings once. He strengthens; and being stronger, generates greater power to work evil. This vampire amongst us is himself so strong in person as twenty men. Cunning more than mortal, for his cunning grown through the ages. He has the aid of necromancy, the divination by the dead, and all the dead that he can come nigh are for him to command."

"The vampire is the devil who can access many powers. Within limitations, he can appear at will when, and where, and in any of the forms that are to him; he can, within his range, direct the elements; the storm, the fog, the thunder; and he can vanish and come unknown. How then are we to begin our strike to destroy him? How shall we find his where; and having found it, how can we destroy?"

"My friends, this is much; it is a terrible task that we undertake. The consequence if we fail in this fight is that he will surely win; and then where end we? To fail here, is not mere life or death. It is that we become like him; that we henceforward become foul things of the night like him, without heart or conscience, preying on the bodies and the souls of those we love best. But we are face to face with duty; and in such case must we shrink? For me, I say, no; but then I am old. You two are yet young, you may have seen sorrow; but there are fair days yet in store. What say you?"

"We are with you, Van Helsing. It is the most pressing case that we have ever engaged, and we realize that the lives of many more people than us depend upon our success. Our lack is the whereabouts of the lair of this creature. Surely it must be close to his most recent actions?" Said Sherlock, leaning further towards the Professor, hanging on the edge of his seat and to every word.

"The vampire lives on and cannot die by mere passing of the time; he can flourish when that he can fatten on the blood of the living." Van Helsing riddled.

"The poor souls lodged in St. Olave's provide a larder for his fuel. He must be close to his source!" Said I.

"You should be right, my friend. His vital faculties grow exhausted and appear they refresh themselves when his special nutrient is plenty. But he cannot flourish without this diet. We have seen amongst us he can even grow younger; that he throws no shadow; he makes in the mirror no reflection, as again Jonathan observed in his journal. He has the strength of many of his hand, witness again Jonathan when he shut the door against the wolves. The vampire can transform himself into a wolf, as we gather from the ship arrival in Whitby. All those years ago, when he tears open the dog; he can be as bat, as Madam Mina saw him on the window at Whitby, and as friend John saw him fly from this so near house, and as my old friend Quincey saw him at the window of the unfortunate Miss Lucy. He can come in the mist which he creates, that noble ship's captain proved him of this; but, from what we know, the distance he can make this mist cover is limited, and it can only be around himself. The vampire can become so small, we ourselves saw, Dracula slip through a hairbreadth space at Lucy's tomb door. He can, when once he finds his way, come out from anything or into anything, no matter how close it is bound or even fused up with fire, solder you call it. He can see in the dark, no minor power this, in a world which is one half shut from the light."

"This is important that we know these things, but they are useless if we do not find him. He has given us only three more nights to succeed in our task." Said Sherlock.

"Ah but hear me through. He can do all these things, yet he is not free. Nay: he is even more prisoner than the slave of the galley, than the madman in his cell. Dracula cannot go where he lists; he who is not of nature has yet to obey some of nature's laws, why we know not. He may enter nowhere at the first, unless there be someone in the household who bid him to come. Though afterwards he can come as he pleases. His power ceases, as does that of all evil things, at the coming of the day. Only at certain times can he have limited freedom. If he is not at the place of his lair, he can only change himself at noon or at exact sunrise or sunset. These things are we told, and in this record of ours we have proof by inference. Thus, whereas he can do as he will within his limit, when he has his earth-home, his coffin-home, his hell-home, the place unhallowed, as I found when he went to the grave of the suicide at Whitby. It is said, too, that he can only pass running water at the slack or the flood of the tide. Then there are things which so afflict him he has no power, as the garlic that we know of. As for things sacred, such as this symbol, my crucifix. There are others, too, which I shall tell you of, lest in our seeking we may need them. The branch of wild rose on his coffin keeps him he moves not from it; a sacred bullet fired into the coffin kill him so that he becomes truly dead; and as for the stake through him, we know already of its peace; or the cut-off head that provides rest. I have seen it with my own eyes." Van Helsing halted his speech, paused, and gazed at us both before saying.

"Thus, when we find the habitation of this man-that-was, we can confine him to his coffin and destroy him, if we obey what we know. But he is clever."

"But where will this coffin lie? Where is his place of rest? Professor, where will we find his lair!" I asked.

"The answer is not with me or you. We will visit the Harker's, because they know of it, whether they yet realize the fact, it will soon be discovered."

31

THE BREADCRUMB

Through the clouded refraction of the glass, the white face of the clock on the mantle showed forty minutes after mid-day. We had exhausted our conversation and fact sharing. Between us, there was little energy remaining. Even Sherlock looked fatigued. His mind whirring about his head together with the range of possibilities, a roulette wheel of logical solutions. My fear was that there was no logic to be found behind this.

"We will visit with Mina and Jonathan today?" Van Helsing interrupted the brief silence.

"Yes, and with the boy, Quincey. We shall do so after lunch." Sherlock replied.

"Oh, I had been hoping we would remove the boy from this, but I recognize that the danger is upon him too." Said Helsing. He paused for a moment and brushed his brow lightly with the handkerchief taken from his top jacket pocket.

"Mina is the key to the door. As you have known from my notes, if she can, by our hypnotic trance, tell what the Count sees and hears, is it not truer that he who has hypnotized her first. He who has drunk of her very blood and makes her drink of his, should, if he will, compel her mind to disclose to him that which she knows? Indeed, Jonathan is within the same purview of inspection." Sherlock nodded agreement.

"That is why we have secured them in a hotel, away from our dealings. Although it is likely, as my good friend Watson pointed out to me this morning, Dracula will have the eyes of others on our activities. We need to engage Mina to reveal the secrets as her subconscious may allow, for our location of the lair of Dracula depends upon it."

"Then, what we must do is to prevent this; we must keep Mina and Jonathan always ignorant of our intent, and so they cannot tell what they know not. This is a painful task! Oh, so painful that it breaks my heart to think of doing the same as I did those years ago; but it must be. When today we meet, I must tell them that for a reason which we will not speak they all must not more be of our council but simply guarded by us." He wiped his forehead again, which had broken out in profuse perspiration at the thought of repeating the pain which he might have to inflict upon the poor soul already so tortured.

I knew it would be some sort of comfort to him if I told him. We also had come to the same conclusion; for at any rate, it would take away the pain of doubt. I told him, and the effect was as I expected. He calmed. Outside of the lodgings a cab drew to a halt and Inspector Lestrade ran into the building, brushing aside the attention of Mrs. Hudson and ascending the stairs to enter our chamber some seconds before she caught him.

"Sherlock, I could not stop this man." Mrs. Hudson panted as she followed closely behind him into the room.

"It is alright, Mrs. Hudson. I am sure that Inspector

Lestrade will make an apology before he moves any further. Inspector?"

"Well, yes. My apologies, madam, I have urgent police business with Sherlock." Mrs. Hudson gave a quick huff of breath and a shrug of her shoulders before closing the door on her exit.

"Pull up a chair from the table and set it beside us, Inspector."

"We have had evidence that is fresh to me this morning," said Lestrade, still panting from his rapid climb. "A passenger who arrived at Fenchurch Street station onboard a Great Eastern train about eleven forty last night declared that he heard a heavy thud, as of a body striking the roof of the carriage in which he was travelling. The event occurring just before the train arrived at the station. He made a report of it. At the time there was a dense thick fog, however, and the searchers could see nothing thereabouts at the time of the incident. By morning, the fog had cleared, and a woman's emaciated body found on the embankment. It was lying wide of the metals upon the right hand of the track as one goes eastward at a point close to the station. The body being broken in many places. It could only have come on the line from a fall, but there are no buildings or bridges in the path. The woman's corpse was in the same condition as the others that we have observed as victims of Dracula. Bearing the same marks on the neck and having little in content of blood within. Why, whatever is the matter with Mr. Holmes?"

Sherlock had the look of a bloodhound about him.

"Inspector, have you identified the woman?"

"No, we do not know who she is, only by the uniform of her employ."

"The uniform? Let me say that the woman is small in stature, in her late twenties, reddish hair, perhaps tied to be placed under a cap. The uniform being that of a nurse."

"Remarkable Holmes! That is the description."

"No so remarkable as expected. I fear it is the night nurse of St. Olave's. taken and disposed of by the Count, one Mary Maroney. The nurse so described to us at the workhouse, on duty the night of the murder of Bill Guy. We need to know her home address."

"You have the body held, inspector?" Asked Van Helsing.

"Yes, it will be at the morgue, at St. George's in the East, they will carry out an autopsy."

"We must be there, before they make any mark! Our visit with the Harker's must wait."

The cab that had brought Lestrade to our door was standing where it had stopped earlier on the street, we took to it, the four of us, and headed to the mortuary within the grounds of the Church of St George in the East at 14 Cannon Street Road, the East End of London. Van Helsing clutched a small brown leather surgical bag tightly to his chest. It had seen some life and plenty of death in its time; the handle worn, and the scuffed hide splitting around the bulging seams, the initials upon it read A. V. H. M. D., D. Ph., D. Lit.

We approached the mortuary, a small brick shed, and Lestrade knocked and immediately opened the door. I am of the medical profession and through my service in the field used to the awful scent of the decay of the dead. This would not compensate me for the aroma that exuded from the door when the air within that building expanded into the cold. Through the opening we caught sight of several bodies, wrapped in sheet, each on a wooden rack stacked one upon the other. A tall man approached the doorway and ushered Lestrade backwards into the yard and to its natural ventilation.

“Well, well, Inspector Lestrade, what brings you here?” Said the well-dressed tall man, sporting a full, healthy beard and mustache, which was trimmed to hang below remarkably high cheekbones and piercing blue eyes.

“Ah, Dr. Blackwell, good to see you again, after all that trouble with the Ripper cases those years ago.”

“Yes, an unfortunate series of events, which disappointingly had no resolution.”

“Maybe because I was not consulted.” Said Sherlock.

“Not now, Sherlock.” Lestrade halted the line of conversation, continuing, “Dr. Blackwell, an unidentified body was delivered here this morning.”

“Only amongst ten others, Inspector!”

“The particular one that we are looking for is that of a young woman, dressed in a nurse’s uniform.”

“Yes, I examined the woman. Unusual death.”

“Unusual? Why, what did you find?”

"Evidence of a fall, many broken bones, radius, tibia, fibula, and multiple vertebral fractures. I would say caused from a fairly high fall, maybe two stories or more. But this was not the cause of death, and that was more of a fact than my opinion. The woman was evidently dead before the fall. There was no blood in her body, not one drop. Nothing evident on her clothing or from the injuries caused. Most peculiar, most peculiar indeed."

"She was obviously carried or thrown to the place that we found her. Did you observe any unusual marks upon her?"

"The two small punctures on the side of her neck, the other marks were all consistent with the effects of fall."

"Can we examine the body?" I asked. At that, Dr. Blackwell shook his head and shrugged his shoulders.

"Unfortunately, a strange event occurred before your arrival. The body removed from its place while I stepped out of the building earlier today, only moments before your arrival. Finishing my examination, I noticed a sudden quiet fall on the grounds. All the birds fell silent, and the branches on the trees stopped their sway. The light disappeared; the day became black. I stepped outside into a full and dense, cold green-yellow fog. The visibility reduced to a point that I could not see my hand before my eyes. I became disoriented, and it took some judgement to find my way back to the doorway. On re-entering the morgue, I found someone must have visited while I was gone and made away with the body of the nurse, together with its uniform. The gown and sheet covering laid on the floor in the center of the room. I do not know who took the corpse or for what reason, I saw no-one, and no other body disturbed."

There was no doubt in any of our minds that the identity of the young woman was certainly that of Mary Maroney and that she was yet another victim of Dracula or his servants. The question was, why was the body removed and where had it been taken? Would it rise again like those described in Jonathan Harker's Journal and as described by Van Helsing? We needed to visit with the Harker's at their hotel before nightfall and so returned to the cab. The thought spurred Sherlock to consider the resting places of Seward and Godalming. Were they subject of the transformation that had affected others?

"Inspector, when you have opportunity, send men to examine the graves of Seward and Godalming."

"You think something ill may have occurred, Sherlock?"

"There is mention in the journal's action that we must guard against; I shall confer with the Professor."

32

TO THE HOTEL

The bells of neighborhood timekeepers tolled; their chimes born on the air and swirling around the streets announcing to all who could hear that it was now three o'clock in the afternoon. We arrived at the hotel in Victoria. An impressive building. The Great Western Hotel is perhaps London's largest and most sumptuous hotel and forms a façade of the railway station adjacent. A pleasing stucco-fronted block of five stories with seven story towers at its corners. It stands tall, dominating and overlooking the street. An architectural beauty, in a style reminiscent of the French Renaissance.

Winter was on us in its first throw, the temperature growing colder by the day, with no prospect of any warmth for the next three months. Huddled in their overcoats, scarves and gloves, a bustle of unsuspecting souls wandered busily about their business through the mists carried by the damp, through the narrow streets. Unaware of the terror that lay in their midst.

In my mind, we were no closer to finding the lair than we were yesterday. I had so many reasons to believe in my friend's subtle powers of reasoning, and extraordinary energy in action, that I felt he must have some solid grounds for the assured and easy demeanor with which he treated the singular mystery which he had been called upon to fathom. Once only had I known him to fail, with the King of Bohemia and of the Irene Adler photograph; but when I looked back to the weird business of the Sign of Four, and the extraordinary circumstances connected with the Study in Scarlet, I felt it would be a strange complication of events indeed which he could not unravel. I hoped now that this meeting with the Harker's would bring us the impetus that we need.

The entrance to the hotel lobby held grand embellishments of tiles and decoration. Accessed through a singular revolving door, through which we took turns in navigating into the luxurious tiled foyer. We confirmed the room and our business and continued on our way. The Harker's were sequestered on the seventh floor of the end tower closest to the street and had kept themselves secure by taking the cloves of the garlic plant and attaching them above all entry points. We approached the door to the room. Sherlock knocked upon the door. Jonathan Harker opened it.

"It is time, Mr. Harker, for us to fathom our next step. We need Mina's help to do so. May we enter?' Said Sherlock.

"Of course, Mr. Holmes. Please come within. Mina is in the bedroom. She has had about her a quietness today."

Sherlock, Lestrade and I were allowed entry. Jonathan, catching sight of his old friend, leapt towards him in one stride, brushing aside Lestrade and Sherlock as he did so.

"Professor! I am so happy to see you. We are now so desperate for your help, just as we were all those years ago. The Count is back, and he seeks vengeance on us all! We celebrated too soon this year with our visit and cursed ourselves with it." Jonathan released his grip on the Professor, his expression turning from delight to concern. They marched towards the room where Mina was resting. The suite held two bedrooms. The boy,

Quincey, remained silent and seated at the window, looking down onto the street below. In his hand a pocket watch, making time with a loud ticking which could be heard from some distance.

"It is very good to be seeing you, my young man. Mina is well?"

"Yes, Mina is well, but she is worried for us all and it is playing on her health. She has been silent on all matters these last few days. I wish we had not come to London for all of this. I miss Whitby and the clean sea air. The atmosphere in this city cannot be good for anyone's constitution. What with the fogs and the smoke."

"There is little choice, Jonathan. We hear of Seward and Godalming. There is a vengeance in play, and we are all part of it. More than us, however, there have been others in London that have paid the Count's price, I am sure many more than we know of."

"I think back to our celebrations this last summer and our visit to Transylvania. We must have brought these events back upon ourselves! I am minded believing that the monster followed on with our return. Do you have similar thoughts?"

"My opinion is that the Count's plans are built upon many

months of preparation, and that he has been setting those in motion in London for some time. He would need to find a building that was suitable for his purpose, that would take time and planning. What resources did he have to put in place? And we are not sure how he has travelled. Maybe he has used the water again. The river is close at hand and has many large buildings around it." Said the Professor.

"Jonathan, we need to speak with both you and Mina together." Interrupted Sherlock at the same moment, introducing Inspector Lestrade.

"This is Inspector Lestrade of Scotland Yard. He is helping direct the search for the murderer. He knows Dracula is the most dangerous of creatures. At the moment, the police are investigating a large area of London for buildings that would be viable as the lair of the monster. We know from the journals that Mina has a subconscious link with the mind of the creature that we seek. She can provide information that we cannot access ourselves. Van Helsing desires to engage in the hypnotizing of Mina as he did before, revealing these clues to assist us. We only have two more nights after the one before us now. Then Dracula will engage with us. And I fear that if we do not discover where he lies before then he will destroy us all as he has promised, and then many others at his will."

"Hypnotize? But you cannot again, you know of the toll placed on my dear wife when we first went through this difficulty. I am worried. The strain and the effort will be too much for her now. There are the times of sunrise and sunset are moments of peculiar freedom, when her old self can be manifested with no controlling force subduing or restraining her. This mood begins some half hour or more before the sunrise or sunset, and lasts till either the sun is high, or whilst the clouds are still aglow with the rays streaming above the horizon. At first there is a sort of negative condition, as if some knot were loosened, and then the absolute freedom quickly follows; when, however, the freedom ceases, the change-back or relapse comes quickly, preceded only by a spell of warning silence. It is such a harsh impact upon her constitution. And what more, we have Quincy to care about!"

"Mr. Harker, you know I would not ask or even attempt such invasion if it did not need to be made. It is the only way we have of getting a step ahead in this encounter."

"This criminal has not a full man-brain. He is clever and cunning and resourceful; but he is not of man-stature as to brain. Yes, it is the dangerous time to be prying into the mind of this monster, but it needs to be done, and quickly. While we have the advantage. You know that Mina's safety is our solemnest duty. We go into danger, to which she is, or may be, more liable than any of us to face the retribution of the monster that we face." Said Van Helsing, mopping his brow.

Jonathan knew that he and the fate of his family rested again on the shoulders of his wife. He directed us with reluctance to the first bedroom. The blinds in the room were open, the light of the evening was fading, and Mina was sitting on the edge of her bed with her head in her hands, the elbows resting on her thighs. She raised her head, her hair parted, and her eyes set upon Van Helsing. Immediately, Mina's expression issued a wry smile containing both happiness and fear within it. We others formed a semi-circle around to the rear of the Professor.

"It is good to see you, my friend, but I wish it were not so. I also understand what your business is around me and I will be part of it, no matter the cost. Forgive me Jonathan." She said. Her smile knowing more than we were aware.

.

33

THE HYPNOSIS

"Yes, I want you to hypnotize me!" Mina, without hesitation, continued. "Do it before the night fully arrives, for I know it is before that time I can speak and speak freely. Be quick, for the time will pass quickly!" she remained seated on the edge of her bed. Without a word, Van Helsing motioned her to position herself comfortably and to look directly at him. Sherlock, Lestrade and Jonathan remained on the edge of the room. The Professor pulled a chair to be close and in front of her, opened up his surgical case. He had evidently been preparing and had his method made up. He took out a bottle of some tincture, shook it with vigor, opened it, and placed the neck of the bottle under Mina's nose.

"Breathe Mina, breathe in the scent deeply, it will relax your body and your mind, you will feel a calm come to your thoughts, and it will add fortitude to your subconscious."

Mina took in several deep breaths of the vapor, a sweet-smelling herb of an origin only the Professor knew. Almost immediately, her shoulders relaxed, and her breathing became slower and deeper. After sealing and replacing the bottle of potion in his bag, Van Helsing began his business. Staring at her, he made passes in front of her, reaching over the top of her head downward, with each hand fluttering before her. One after the other.

Mina gazed at him with a hard stare for a few minutes, during which my heartbeat became in my mind the loudest sound in the room, like a trip hammer. My emotions surged, and a shiver hit my soul, for I felt that some crisis was at hand. Gradually her eyes tired and closed, and she sat, stock still; only by the gentle rhythmic heaving of her bosom could one know she was alive. The Professor made a few more passes and then stopped, and I could see that his forehead was covered with great beads of perspiration from the effort of his concentration.

Mina opened her eyes; but she did not seem the same woman. There was a remote and far-away look in the dark centers of the blue, and her voice had a sad dreaminess which was new to me. Raising his hand to impose silence, the Professor motioned to me to bring Sherlock, Lestrade, and Jonathan closer. They came on tiptoe, first closing the room door behind them, and stood at the foot of the bed, looking on. Mina appeared not to see them. Van Helsing's voice broke the stillness in a low-level tone which would not break the current of her thoughts.

"Where are you?" The answer came neutrally:

"I do not know. Sleep has no place it can call its own." For several minutes, there was silence. Mina sat rigid, and the Professor stood staring at her fixedly; the rest of us hardly dared to breathe. The room was growing darker; without taking his eyes from Mina's face, Professor Van Helsing motioned me to pull up the blind. I did so, and the day was to be just departing us. The sun setting over the rooftops of London, and the last of the rosy light seemed to diffuse itself through the evening mist and into the room, casting our shadows on to the wall behind. In the instant the Professor spoke again:

"Where are you now?"

The answer came dreamily, but with intention; it was as though she were interpreting something. I have heard her use the same tone when reading from the journals.

"I do not know. It is all strange to me!"

"What do you see?"

"I can see nothing; it is all dark."

"What do you hear?" I could detect the strain in the Professor's patient voice.

"There is the lapping of water. It is gurgling rather than the sound of the waves on the beach. I can hear them on the outside of the thick wall, calmer than an ocean, stronger than a stream."

"Then you are not on a ship or a boat?" We all looked at each other, trying to glean something each from the other. We were afraid to think. The answer came quick:

"No, I am in a substantial building, a new building. I can smell the construction. The dust of the brick and timber, then above me a tower."

“Are you in a room, is it small or large?”

“It is dark. I can see a flickering. A flame. On a wall close by, illuminating the wall. The room is small, the ceiling higher.”

“What more?”

“The tower is square, it has brick sides, there laid stone about it too. Narrow steps curve upwards from the entrance to the room at their foot. A single door into a small windowless room. That is where I am. Now I see the ceiling of the room more clearly, not a solid or flat surface, but a machine, steel panel, bolts, pistons, and mechanical movement. For now, it is motionless, but will soon be brought to life once the day begins. Held still during the hours of darkness.”

“What else do you notice, any sounds?”

“The noise of people stamping overhead as they run about their business. There is the creaking and metallic sound of chains, the hiss of steam, and automated mechanical noise of pulleys. I can hear the bustle of the end of the day outside, footsteps on metal grates.”

“What more of your surroundings? Are you alone?”

"No, there are others here, two more that are silent and motionless. I think I know well."

"Who are they?"

"They are, I cannot quite see, but…I am still, oh, so still. It is like death, but I am to awake soon, the darkness is calling me, and I have much work to do!" The voice faded away into a deep breath as if one sleeping, and the open eyes closed again.

By this time, the sun had sunk from the day, and we were all in the darkness of night. Van Helsing placed his hands on Mina's shoulders and laid her head down softly on her pillow. She lay like a sleeping child for a few moments, and then, with a long sigh, awoke and stared in wonder to see us all around her. "I talked in my sleep. Was it of help as the times before?" was all she said. She seemed, however, to know the situation without telling, though she was eager to know what she had told. The Professor repeated the conversation, and she said:

"Then there is not a moment to lose: we must find this place!" and she lurched upright but the Professor's calm voice called her to lie again. He then continued.

"My friends, it is now known that the Count lies within a building close to the water. That may help with our search. My thoughts are setting themselves on the river and on the industrial buildings that line its banks."

"The river runs in the center of the area that we seek the lair. The most unpleasant of waterways, a harbor for many harmful by-products of humanity, but a suitable location for nefarious activities. Industries, wharves, and docks line the banks like sharpened teeth in a jawbone. It will be difficult to locate the building from the information that we have, do not you think, Holmes?" Said I.

"Let us place the facts that we have together and then narrow our search. We are closer now to our target than when we started the day. We have no time to spare." Said Sherlock.

34

THE TIGHTENING GRIP

“Watson, we need to return to Baker Street, before the night draws closer to its peak.”

Spinning quickly around on his heels to face Van Helsing, Sherlock continued.

“Professor, you must stay here and ensure that this family is safe this night.”

"Yes, I will stay. If that is acceptable to you all?"

"That would be welcome. We can revisit our journey of last summer and prepare ourselves for what is coming. It will be good to share the evening with a good friend, it will give us all the greater safety." Said Jonathan. Sherlock followed quickly with instructions to the Inspector.

"Lestrade, we have a direction in which the building is close to the water. Here it must be on the river. You should direct your team tomorrow to focus on buildings on the Thames from London Bridge Wharf eastwards, both on the northern and southern banks to Rotherhithe Station. Any buildings that also have a tower."

"Yes, my people will concentrate on the waterfront on both shores as soon as the day breaks."

My friend smiled and laid his hand on my arm. "I think, Watson, that I shall resume that course of tobacco-poisoning which you have so often and so justly condemned," said he. "With your permission, all, we will now return to Baker Street, for I am not aware that any new factor is likely to come to our notice here. I will turn the facts over in my mind, Lestrade, and should anything occur to me I will certainly communicate with you and the Harker's. In the meantime, I wish you all a good evening. We shall reconvene here at twelve noon tomorrow to lay out our plan."

We bid our farewells for the night and left the Hotel. The street outside was dark, and the bustle of the day had expired. We stood to examine the scene before hailing a cab. The street and pavement damp with footsteps that had carried the effort of the day upon them. On seating ourselves within the cab, Sherlock took no time to precede to dissect the hypnotism of Mina in greater detail.

"What do you make of this Watson, what of the location of the lair?"

I understood that this was my friend's way of proving some point of my missing a vital part of what he had discovered. I could do nothing but play along, because there would be some strange small part that would prove important to the whole. If the streets allowed, there were twenty minutes between Victoria and Baker Street. Sherlock remained still, a small curl on the edge of his lips as I outlined what I had noticed.

"There seems to me that the hypnosis contained a confirmation that we are seeking the Count within the correct parameters that we have laid out. The first point that we should seek is a building with at least one wall close to the river. A building that has a tower above a low room of some sort, maybe a basement. The industry, perhaps close to a steam-driven machine. The wharves are full of such machinery, used for lifting, pounding, sawing, grinding and such like, the question being how to separate them towards what we seek."

"Very good, Watson, but there is one small piece that you may have missed.'

"Ahh, the small piece!"

"Yes, Watson, always the small piece. Mina's hypnosis revealed that the building she was speaking of was of new construction. Most of the buildings that lay within our radius are old and have a history that has remained untouched for decades. Then, wc need to focus upon those buildings in the search area which are recently built or renovated. That surely will narrow our suspects."

"We should then only consider the wharves that are in direct contact with the waters of the river as a priority Holmes. That should completely narrow our review further."

"Not only that, Watson, it was a low tide this afternoon,

we should also eliminate the buildings which are affected most by this lowering of the depth of the river. Only those who keep contact with the low tide should remain as candidates."

We arrived at 221B with a revived hope that the area of our interest had reduced. The cab slowed to be still against the front door. Gathered within the mist that was already forming for the night were a group of half a dozen of the 'Baker Street detective police force' as Holmes described them. They were the dirtiest and most ragged street urchins that one could ever clap eyes upon. The group, employed by Sherlock and had been so since my reported case of 'A Study in Scarlet'. They were very efficient in the gathering of information of a type that relationship with the gutter society of London's back streets could only discover. The same back streets that Dracula was frequenting with his purpose. These stragglers of society can access alleys, cellars, and doors that most would steer clear, in fear of harm.

"Wiggins, come now to the apartment, and I shall discuss your endeavors. The rest of you must wait in the street." John Wiggins, the eldest of the gang, a brown-haired skinny youth taller than the others and obviously accepted as their leader, stepped forward and followed us into the apartment. Mrs. Hudson looked on with disbelief and disgust as she held the door ajar.

“Have you any luck with what I have asked you to find?”

“No, sir, we hain’t,” said Wiggins.

“I hardly expected you would. Let me provide a smaller area for your task. Watson, pass the Survey map of Southwark and Bermondsey if you please.”

I found the map amongst a pile of papers wedged in the hat stand. A common place for such an item, I mused to myself before handing it to Sherlock. He took it to the breakfast table and pressed it flat with the palm of each hand. I placed a sharpened pencil in the center of the map for his use before he could ask. He glanced at me with a wry smile, as if to message that I was catching on to his thoughts. Which I was not. He knew that, of course.

“Let us mark what we know, on this map.”

Sherlock set the map and flattened it with care. Then with rapid motion sketched the following points with an ‘X’, citing them aloud as he did so.

“The murdered passenger, Bill Guy, Bermondsey Street,

close to the Church of Mary Magdalen."

"St. Olave's workhouse on Tooley Street. Used as a larder to fuel their wanton activities."

"The home address of the nurse, from which she must have been taken; Lestrade informed me it was at the Red Lion Court, a small attic apartment, close to the railway goods depot."

"The location of the dropped body of the night nurse, on the railroad embankment, close to the station."

"The Mortuary at St. George in the East. Where the body of the nurse disappeared."

"The National Mint, the origin of the newly forged sovereign found on Bill Guy."

"Southwark Park, the place of the attacks by the Dr. Man upon children."

Seeing all the points laid out, he then drew upon it with a steady pencil line that formed a large sweeping oval that enclosed the marks that he had placed. He then looked at the area captured within it and next to the water, a smaller, stretched oval appeared. "Now, I have better information to help you find what we seek."

Sherlock stared at the ceiling and called out the following facts, all emerging from the hypnosis of madam Mina:

"The building that we are looking for contains a tower. It sits with at least one side facing the water. It is an active building, but only during the day when the mechanisms within it operate. There are metal steps close-by and industrial engines that operate by steam power, look for signs of delivery of coal."

"Well, governor, there's still a lot to be looking for."

"Also, pay heed to any strange happenings about an area. You must keep on until we find something that fits all the parts we seek. Unusual activities may take place during darkness, sudden fog, or mists or strange sounds like the howling of dogs. Here are your wages." He handed Wiggins one shilling for each of the group.

"So, off you go, and come back with a better report next time." Sherlock instructed.

Wiggins waved his hand and scampered downstairs. He rejoined the group as they hurried through the street. All together, scurrying like so many rats, we heard their shrill voices fade into the dark, wet grey distance.

"There's more work to be got out of one of those little beggars than out of a dozen of the force," Holmes remarked. "The mere sight of an official-looking person seals men's lips. These youngsters, however, go everywhere and hear everything. They are as sharp as needles, too; all they crave is organization."

"Holmes, it is nearing the time that Dracula will become active again."

"Make haste, Watson, prepare the defense of the openings of this building. We have only two days more to discover the home of the Count."

35

THE FINDING

Saturday morning appeared with a frost at the window, a pattern as individual as the lines on one's thumb. My sleep was again as calm as the one before, although this day had over me a feeling of foreboding. We had made a dent in the investigation; I could know that. Sherlock was again at the breakfast before me and had at his hand a stack of the morning papers. The room was silent but for the ticking of the clock, which brought nothing more to me than the approaching of the next night. The last hours that we would have before the wrath of the monster would be released upon us all. For a moment it took me in thought.

"Watson, you have a look of a faraway traveler about you today!"

"Well, I should say Homes, we have made much progress, but we seem to be at the same distance from our destination. Our proceedings have done little to advance the investigation. The proceedings marked, however, by incidents which have left the most sinister impression upon my mind."

"Watson, do you doubt in my methods? Those which have proven to be the undoing of many adversaries."

"No so much sherlock, the man we chase is a monster, a clever one at that. He takes much of your energy, and I can see it drain. You recovered from all your exertions that tolled you in the spring, and I am concerned that this effort will draw you backwards in health."

Earlier this year Holmes's iron constitution showed some symptoms of giving way in the face of constant hard work of a most exacting kind, aggravated, perhaps, by occasional indiscretions of his own. In March, Dr. Moore Agar, of Harley Street, whose dramatic introduction to Holmes I may someday recount, gave positive injunctions that the famous private agent lay aside all his cases and surrender himself to complete rest if he wished to avert an absolute breakdown. The state of his health was not a matter in which he himself took the faintest interest, for his mental detachment was absolute, but he was induced at last, on the threat of being permanently disqualified from work, to give himself a complete change of scene and air.

“Watson, it has been a long period between that episode and where we are now. I am invigorated by the immensity of the challenge we are facing. Today, as you know, has left us no time but to identify the location. Wiggins will make his report this morning. Lestrade will finish up his search of buildings and we will visit with the Harker’s hoping to discover the location.”

“I hope that this is the case today Holmes.”

“Let us take to the morning papers and seek reports that may help secure the start of the day, before we make our way to the hotel.”

We spread the papers on the table, and we took turns in pulling the pages of various editions. The London Gazette held one of such interest.

“This article strikes me of a particular importance Holmes, it says the industries around St. Saviour’s dock are finding several workers are missing each day from their employment. Industrial wharves of Horsleydown, Coventry's and Cole's being most affected, with entire night shifts of workers missed. The total not returning for work has grown to over two dozen over the last three days. The replacements to those missing similarly disappear, leading to malicious gossip of superstitious influence shared between the working folk of the area."

Sherlock picked up the map and the drawn circle upon it and turned to the table. We searched the banks of the Thames for the wharves named in the article.

"This is good work, Watson. Look at the location on the map. Indiscriminate it is not. These places are on the south side and closer to St. Olave's."

"Above the line of the high tide."

"The water would not have lapped against the wall as Mina reported in her hypnosis. Then, what more than those buildings be, but nothing more than larders for the activities of the vampires. A place to pick and satisfy their blood needs upon those unsuspecting souls. But, then close-by to the lair no-doubt."

At that moment there was a sharp rap on the door and a loud exclamation. After traveling the distance of the stairs, Mrs. Hudson appeared at our apartment with a look of disgust on her face.

“Sherlock, one of your helpers has appeared, one of those...untidy urchins.”

“By all means, show him in. It must be Wiggins with his report Watson. Let us hope he has news so we might close the net tighter.”

“I would ask him to remove his shoes, but he has none.” Replied Mrs. Hudson. Wiggins entered the room and eyed the breakfast table.

“Wiggins, I see you may be in need of some food.”

“Yes, sir.”

“Then please help yourself.”

“Thank you, sir! May I take some for the rest of my fellows?”

“Yes, you may, as much as you can carry.”

For a moment, we threw the map to one side while the bedraggled youth pushed handfuls of whatever remained of the breakfast foods both into his mouth and pockets at the same time.

"Steady on, fellow, you will surely choke if you do not slow. You will take all you need we will be sure of that." I tried to calm the boy.

"So, what about your report?" Asked Sherlock.

"Sir, we set about our task within an hour of your instruction. The start of our search was on the north side of the river at London Bridge Wharf, as marked to be the commencement of the area in question. We studied many of the buildings along that bank. None of them had the form that you had described. On reaching the Tower of London we were to cross to the south side of the river. There is a food stand there that we can get hot potatoes and roasted chestnuts. The new Tower Bridge was in front. Many of us had not climbed to the height of the pedestrian bridge before, so we thought we may get a view as we sighted along the buildings on both sides of the river. Even though the daylight was fading, and the river fog was settling upon its surface, there were many lamps and lights upon the buildings along its banks."

"Excellent thinking Wiggins. Did you see anything from

that vantage?"

"Not from that vantage sir, but upon it!"

"What did you find?"

"The many stairs leading to the walkway were dimly lit, we climbed them with care and on reaching the summit we saw, through the gloom a, strange occurrence. The corridor is of such a span that one cannot easily observe fully the entire length of it. As we stepped on to the start of the structure, we could dimly glimpse bodies lying in strange poses, bowed shoulders, bent knees, heads thrown back and chins pointing upward, with here and there a dark, lack-luster eye turned upon the new-comer as we passed along. Out of the black shadows there glimmered little red circles of light, now bright, now faint, as the burning of small candles waxed or waned in their holders. Of the bodies most lay silent, but some muttered to themselves, and others talked together in a strange, low, monotonous voice, their conversation coming in gushes, and then suddenly tailing off into silence, each mumbling out his own thoughts, and paying little heed to the words of his neighbor."

"At the farther end of the walkway was a small brazier of burning charcoal, beside which on a three-legged wooden stool there sat a small woman, with her jaw resting upon her two fists, and her elbows upon her knees, staring into the fire. Her skin was pale as the moon and her eyes as dark as the night. She stepped to rise, and we could see that she was in the uniform of a nurse, although torn and dirty. Her body corrugated and broken like no other, we could not know how she could stand; the figure came towards us, dragging one foot loose from the leg behind. I have never seen such a sight; turning in fear, we ran from it and did not stop until reaching our lodgings. We secured no meal since we last visited with you."

"Wiggins, you have delivered a piece of gold! Fetch the gang inside so they can eat all they can." At that, Sherlock then cried out.

"Mrs. Hudson, more eggs and sausage if you please!" He took his coat and hat off the rack and dashed towards the door.

"Come on, Watson, we have serious business at hand!"

36

HORROR AT THE GREAT WESTERN

Sherlock exited onto the street from 221B in full flight, disappearing into the gloom of the developing fog, bellowing, filling the space between buildings. I chased afterwards and after catching him after a considerable amount of steps, breathlessly gasping enough of a cry to hail a cab. Exhausted, drawing in the cold damp winter air to regain my breath and feeling its sting on my throat and lungs did nothing for my recovery. Hiding my strain to disguise my lack of stamina, I panted in shallow breaths. Sherlock smiled as he did, of course, observe the condensate I created and its frequency. His constitution, in contrast, showed no such strain. We Climbed into the cab, and took our seats, directing the driver to go quickly to the Great Western Hotel at Victoria. There we would meet with the Harker's, Van Helsing and Lestrade. The arrangement was due at twelve noon, so we had three hours to make the twenty-minute journey. For once we were ahead of the clock. Sherlock was positively beaming at the report from Wiggins. The scheme of things, just as he had imagined. We had made the step ahead of Dracula. The plan would develop, and there was time for us to do so.

"Watson, I am satisfied that we have the location."

"Which is Sherlock?" I said, still panting.

"The most central to the events, not upon the banks of our most odorous river but within it. Think Watson. Where would the most precise pin in the middle of our balloon be?"

"In the river? Then the Tower Bridge, Sherlock? How can that be the point, it is a bridge only? The activities within the pedestrian walkways result from the vampire's need for blood, a living reservoir. Are they not?"

"Indeed, it is a bridge, and being its primary function, it is to many in this city the only function that it holds. The only occurrence that they require a use of the structure is to pass over it as a bridge. The victims held within its corridor are there by design, a ready source of replenishment and energy for Dracula and his cohorts. As your observation connects."

"Yes, I have that observation Holmes, but what greater use could it carry, it is still, after all, only a bridge?"

"Oh, my friend, it is much more than a bridge. You recall the hypnosis of Mina. She mentioned the lair was within a new construction, in darkness, with machinery about the space. You recall that the bridge is built recently and upon deep foundations. The structure welcomed to the river only this year. You informed me of that before the commencement of this investigation, and of the seven years that it took to build. The timeline that we are speaking of that connects to the movement of the Count. Its two enormous towers stand over the mechanical rooms and link to the steam powered equipment used to raise the twin bascules. The operation limited to allow ships to pass during the day. At other times, mainly during darkness and out of the hours of industry, the bridge remains quiet and undisturbed, wrapped in the dense cloak of the river fog. He must be there, in the rooms beneath the towers, he must be!"

"Then what of the plan?"

"The plan will arrive, Watson!"

"We need to set out the arrangements for our attack before the night, and Dracula, come upon us."

"We will arrive at the hotel in but a few minutes and set out the facts, as we have them to the others. Then we shall plan a visit to Tower Bridge and the lair that lies beneath. Using all the resources of Scotland Yard together with the knowledge brought to us by Van Helsing we shall corner the beast and his companions for good."

"This will be nothing but a battle, Sherlock!"

"I am prepared Watson." He took out his .450 short-barreled Webley Metropolitan Police revolver from his pocket and waved it about the cab.

"Please, put that away! I have seen the damage it does to the wall of the apartment!"

We carried the rest of the journey through the early morning streets in silence. Holmes remained cold and stern, concentrating on the task at hand. As the gleam of the daylight flashed upon his austere features, I saw his brows were drawn down in thought and his thin lips compressed. I knew the nature of the wild beast we were about to hunt down in the dark jungle of criminal London, but I was well assured, from the bearing of this master huntsman, that he considered this adventure as a most grave one, while the sardonic smile which occasionally broke through his own self-imposed gloom boded little good for the object of our quest.

Victoria Station passed on our left and we turned the corner from Eastbourne Terrace onto Craven Road and the front of the Great Western Hotel. Without warning, the cab came to an abrupt stop; the horse, being disturbed, reared up on its hind legs. Sherlock and I were both thrown forward as the driver struggled to avoid a crowd gathered on the pathway along the main entrance. Through the grey gloom, we could see an area roped off with many constables guarding the scene. It could only be a crime, and a serious one at that. We jumped out of the cab and entered the crowd, circling a heap on the ground. And so it was, Lestrade appeared, emerging from the swirling mist and the shadows of the crowd. Galloping with urgency towards Sherlock; upon his face a dripping look of shock and fear, the mouth drawn open as a gasp.

37

CURTAINS IN THE WIND

"Last night Sherlock, in the early hours, the most extraordinary and miserable affair has occurred." Lestrade stood directly in front of Holmes.

Sherlock's attention directed itself elsewhere. He gazed skyward at the front of the hotel. His eyes focused on the top floor, the seventh and the room of the Harker's accommodation. The yellow haze cleared for a moment, enough to allow the sight that marked the smashed glazing of the end window. Through the irregular, shattered opening, curtains flapped freely in the breeze, collecting the slight drizzle that was falling from the silvery sky above. On the street, a form recognizable as a body, lay beneath a hastily drawn canvas tarp.

“A most awful event, Sherlock!”

Making my way through to where the body lay. A crumpled and twisted mess. I recognized the color of the hair and the material of the sleeve of the jacket, which were the only parts visible as they extended beyond the edge of the cover draped upon the remains.

“Who was it Lestrade, which one?” Asked Sherlock, returning his focus toward the Inspector.

“Van Helsing. He is still lying on the ground where he fell from the room. We have not moved the body yet. I wanted you to examine it first.”

“The others?”

“We need to go to the room. There is more to find and to tell.”

I soon dispelled the hope that nothing would attach the event to Dracula. Sherlock and Lestrade drew back the sheet that covered the corpse. There was no blood to be seen, no stain on the pavement. Sherlock bent over the body, his hands flitting quickly over the head and chest, then examined the neck. He looked at me and nodded. Holmes paused and grasped Lestrade firmly by the arm just above his elbow, turning him aside from the direction of the crowd.

"Lestrade, did you find any news of the remains of Seward and Godalming?"

"Yes, there is some Sherlock. Both graves disturbed, and the bodies removed."

"Removed or walked!"

"You think that they have risen to be with Dracula?"

"Of that I have now no doubt. The resurrection of the dead to take on the form of a vampire is a reality. Van Helsing told us directly, and we have seen the evidence. There is only one way to be sure that this does not follow for poor Van Helsing. There is only one way, you must disable the corpse before this evening. Task the forensic doctor to remove the heart and destroy it by fire."

"I do not know if that can be done, Sherlock! There are protocols."

"We must do it Inspector; else we will find another enemy in our midst."

"I will instruct it, and I can only hope that it is. First, we need to go to the room, there is much more to this."

Lestrade ran to the entrance and led us both to the room via the stairs. After seven flights we arrived, I was breathless for the second time today. On arriving at the door of the room, a solitary uniformed police officer guarding entry met us. Who in identifying Lestrade ushered us within.

What greeted us was a room now strewn with tables, chairs, and clothing, all the items that had made the room of the highest quality thrown about. The blue velvet curtains of the main window being blown inside, and then sucked out of the jagged window opening. The crisp air buffeting the interior space, reinforcing the chill to the spine that the scene set.

One realized the fiery energy which underlay Holmes's phlegmatic exterior when one saw the sudden change which came over him from the moment that he entered the fatal hotel room. In an instant he was tense and alert, his eyes shining, his face set, his limbs quivering with eager activity.

“The others?” Asked Sherlock, running across the room from corner to corner, examining the scene with a swiftness I had become accustomed, but which would seem strange to others.

“Yes, what of Jonathan, Mina, and the boy, Quincy?” I interjected.

“No sign of anyone in the room when the first officer arrived after the commotion was reported.” Replied Lestrade. Sherlock still scanning around, his eyes up, down, at the same time walking to the gaping window and its broken frame. He placed his finger on the ends of the splintered wood and examined them with his magnifying lens. Stepping away, his shoes crunched upon the broken glass now inlaid like small diamonds into the carpet beneath his soles. Under the unbroken, but unfastened, window lay a silver crucifix. Sherlock opened the window and poked his head into the weather to glance at the street below. He turned to look back at Lestrade.

“How was the commotion noticed?”

"The crashing of glass disturbed the occupants of the room directly below. Then soon afterwards the body of Van Helsing discovered on the street below."

"How soon?"

"A matter of a few minutes."

"Your men have examined the room? What evidence have they presented?"

"Other than Van Helsing jumped or thrown through the closed window, my men have returned nothing more."

"Elementary Inspector. But only if the investigators do not observe what is plainly in view!"

"Then, you are welcome to discover what you may Sherlock, and I fortunate to receive it."

"My good man, the exit of Van Helsing did not precipitate the damage to the window or its frame. The damage is caused by the entry through from the outside. Notice the direction of the splinters and the glass on the carpet, some distance from the opening. You have also noticed the crucifix at the undamaged window. And looking out of that window directly onto the street below is the position of the fallen Professor. That is the point of his exit."

"Then the Professor jumped from the building?"

"That is something for yet I do not have the answer. However, I fear that is an unlikely scenario as I observe that there are no marks evident upon its sill that would support anyone climbing upon it, and it remains closed. Such a feat to close the window after one makes a jump from it, do not you suppose?"

At that moment, a rustling came from the smaller bedroom. We entered the room in a rush, Sherlock leading, Lestrade and I keeping close behind. The bedroom was that of the boy's; the bed overturned, and clothing strewn about. Pictures and their frames, once on the wall, lay shattered all around. The curtains, still attached to their rail, piled in a heap beneath the window. Sherlock inspected the lock to the sash. It was in place and fixed to be closed; the garlic used as defense to entry was still hanging in its place. The rustling began again; it originated from a pile of bed linen stacked untidily in the room's corner, beside the wardrobe. Sherlock, leaning down with his left arm outstretched, took hold of a corner of the material, and swiftly drew back the top sheet.

38

WITNESS

Lestrade gasped as the sheet flew over Sherlock's head, arching in the air towards the ceiling, as it followed the direction of Sherlock's pull. There, sitting huddled, with his knees under his chin, and holding his father's kukri knife, was the boy, Quincey. He sat stock still, the small fingers of both hands wrapped firmly around the carved bone handle of the weapon, the same weapon that Jonathan had used to dispatch Dracula at their last encounter. The blade was of a shape that I had seen used to terrifying effect by the Gurkha regiment during my service in Afghanistan, a familiar and distinct recurve with a sharp edge.

“My God! The boy!” cried Lestrade.

“They took them, I heard it!” Said Quincey looking at Sherlock, with a face that showed only anger, rather than the anguish that we may have expected from the small boy.

“Who did?” Sherlock replied.

“It was the Lord and the Dr. and some other.”

“Godalming and Seward! They live!”

“Not so Watson, it is not life that they enjoy. They walk and respond to their master’s command.”

“Come, boy, let us get you to a more comfortable place. Pass me that knife before you hurt yourself.” Said Lestrade.

“No, sir, I shall hold this blade. I shall not release my grip from it. I am practiced in its use.”

“Then place the knife back into its sheath and come with us. Are you hurt, boy?” Asked Lestrade.

Quincey pulled the leather sheath for the knife from

beneath his position and placed the long-curved blade back into its holder, the sound of the metal on its leather protector a familiar post battle song.

"No sir, I am not injured."

I took Quincey by his free hand; he clung onto the sheathed knife with the other. I led him through the wreckage and into the main bedroom adjacent. It was as though we had entered a different world. Nothing disturbed, everything remained in its place, a serene interlude to the scene outside. It was the same room that we had left after the Professor's hypnosis of Mina, only hours before. Van Helsing's surgical bag lay open on its side beside the bed, its contents strewn across the floor.

"What of this Sherlock? Is this not the strangest sight?"

"Strange in appearance, but not unexpected, Watson." Sherlock made his examination of the room from where he stood.

"How so?"

"Notice, at the window the garlic remains hanging, at the others it does not. This window would be impenetrable to the vampire from the outside. Also note at the threshold to this room there is sprinkled a wafer of some sort. The same that Van Helsing had used to prevent Dracula entering the circle in Transylvania no doubt."

"Then why did not all shelter in this room? When they knew they would be safe!" Asked the inspector.

"Why indeed, perhaps the boy knows more about this and can tell his story."

Sherlock turned to Quincey, who was now sitting on the bed, in the same spot Mina had lain hypnotized the night before. The boy held the sheathed kukri tightly pressed into his lap, the silence in the room was only broken by the timepiece held in the boy's pocket, a loud ticking that I had noticed before. Quincey bore the good looks of both his parents; his character bore the same resilience and determination.

"Quincey, it is important to tell us all you know about what happened here before your memory sets a different view of the events. Can you do that?"

"Yes sir, I can."

"How did the events of the night unfold?"

"I had retired to bed not long since you left. The Professor was talking to my mother in her room with my father. It was soon that I was asleep in my bed, but then I awoke with a start. I do not know have much time had passed. It was a whisper at my window, but the sound departed before I got to it to look out. There was nothing present, and I returned to my bed. It was then I heard my mother call and the window in the main room opening fully."

"The main window?"

"Yes, I knew it was the main window because it made a scraping sound that I had heard before. Then the voices were in the room. I went to my door softly and listened. Unless my ears deceived me, it was a conversation between my parents, Van Helsing, and another. There was a low, sweet ripple of laughter amongst the voices, which was not theirs. Suddenly, there was then the breaking of the glass, a sound that was followed by a scuffling and silence, then more voices. In fear I turned and pulled the blankets from the storage shelf and hid beneath them with the knife. I became scared and motionless, but I was ready to strike."

"Then the voices, who were they all?"

"I recognized the Lord Godalming and the Dr. Seward. I knew them from our visit to the castle this summer.

There was another, much deeper, I did not know."

"You are sure of that?"

"Yes sir, I know the voices well, they are my uncles, or so I call them."

"What then?"

"My room door opened and things thrown about, the bed overturned. I thought they would come upon me. Where I was hiding. There was no reason for them not to; I gripped the knife, feeling their breath over my head as my hair stood on end. They found my place. There was to be no escape. Until the deep voice shouted."

"You heard what the voice said?"

"Yes, he said. Back, back, to the place!" Quincey hesitated. "There were more words I cannot recall."

"Try my boy."

"Something like, tomorrow night is yours! It was a voice penetrating my mind, forcing me to listen to it, to notice those words!"

"But I did not move. I stayed hidden until you found me, knowing they had been about my hiding place. Why did they leave me? What is about tomorrow? We need to find my mother and father; they will surely intend to hurt them."

"We will find them. Be sure of that!"

Sherlock bent beside the bed and took hold of the open surgical bag left by Van Helsing on the floor. Picking it up, he immediately turned its assorted contents onto the bed. Medical instruments clattered together as they fell into a pile. I recognized and checked them off in my mind. Ear trumpet, a folding magnifying glass, eyedropper, thermometer, a small kit of scalpels, forceps, tweezers and scissors, syringes with needles and probes. There were several leather straps to use as tourniquets or restraints, small glass bottles and slides to collect samples, opiate, cocaine, and adrenaline ampules. All these were standard items that most holding such a bag would carry within it. The items that were not standard therefore stood out and became of utmost interest.

"A small mallet and a set of sharpened wooden stakes, a dissecting saw, a bottle marked 'heilig', the half full bottle of the hypnotizing tincture used on Mina, a box of wafer material, and this small book of notes in Dutch." Said

Sherlock, setting them aside and turning to the Inspector. I could see by Holmes's face that he was much puzzled by something which he had observed. His knitted brows and abstracted eyes would show that his thoughts had gone back once more to the hypnosis of Mina, by which it enacted this tragedy. I felt a creeping of the flesh, and a presentiment of coming horror. Then, breaking free of his thoughts.

"These are the items that we must take with us, Lestrade, if you will allow?"

"If you think they will be of use, then we should."

"Good, now to set out our plan."

"Where do we start?" Asked Quincey.

"You are not coming." Said Lestrade.

"But I fear he must." Added Sherlock as a command.

39

FURIOUS RAMPAGE

We can never be certain of what happened that night at the Hotel. And what movements occurred in the room before Van Helsing's death. I can only surmise the sequence from the pieces that we found, the broken window, the wreckage within the room and the discovery of the boy in hiding. I would place all of this together after the event, attempting to describe the activities as far as the statement from Quincey and the deductions made by Holmes allow.

The positions of the players in the scene would seem to

be set. Mina was in the main room, recovering from the hypnotism. Jonathan and Van Helsing remained in the large bedroom, discussing the plan for the day, which would be on them in a matter of hours. Quincy was asleep in his room. Whether Mina's hand engaged it, or the window of the lounge opened with no obvious physical intervention. Squealing on its runners as it did so, that is what Quincey heard moments after sounds awoke him at his own window.

It must have been by Mina's hand as she must have removed the noxious smelling garlic defense that had laid upon the opening from its hook on the inside and loosened the latch only moments before. I imagine that a dense and sudden fog swirled around the portal. From that moment, I can only vision the moments that ensued.

Suddenly, with a single bound, Dracula leapt into the room, shifting his shape from that of a giant bat into his most youthful image of the last one hundred years. There had never been such a resource of lifeblood at his hands. Partaking of the readily available thick human syrup on a regular occasion would have rejuvenated his ancient cells and his strength. In comparison, the forest wilds of his barren mountain home had never supplied the volume and number of victims as the largest city in England was able. Therefore, he was, in appearance, a man in his twenties, notwithstanding that he had lived for centuries. Standing in front of him Mina, for a moment frozen in shock, smiled. Her eyes widened and fixed upon him in a hypnotic stare. Then, in a single unexpected movement, she welcomed him into her outstretched arms. He came to her, and they embraced.

"You are here!" she cried.

The screeching window drew Jonathan and Professor Van Helsing to the doorway of the bedroom. They looked out onto the embrace; the Count returned their shocked expressions with a grimacing contortion. Dracula's face filled with hate as he faced them. Throwing Mina away and behind him, he moved towards the opening. The invisible shield provided by the holy wafers spread on the floor held him at bay. He laughed in a deep growl.

"You cannot prevent the events that are about to take place, in front of your eyes. You do not realize the control I exert over you all!"

"Mina, come back into the room!" Shouted Jonathan, pleading with her to return to safety. Van Helsing turned and moved towards his surgical bag, spilling some of its contents on the floor before removing from it a silver crucifix, which he clutched in his right hand.

"It is too late Jonathan; she is with me. Mina has been wanting my arms since the first time that we had shared our passion those years ago. She has never been free. We have the strongest of connections deep within our subconscious, reinforced further by the hypnotic intrusion you made earlier today. You think to baffle me, you, with your pale faces in a row, like sheep in a butcher's. I have seen and heard all that you have planned and spoke about. You think you have found my resting place in which to corner me. My revenge is just begun! I can spread it over centuries or release it in moments, and as time is on my side. The girl that you love is mine already; and through her you and others shall yet be mine, my creatures, to do my bidding and to be my jackals when I need to feed."

"Come Jonathan, Dracula is our master, he is the master of us all, come enjoy his empire." Mina said in a gentle, soothing manner in her voice. Her face becoming softer, her cheeks flushed, her lips looking fuller. Jonathan stepped towards the entrance but was held by the Professor, who shouted.

"No, you will leave us now!" Van Helsing, pushing Jonathan to one side and holding the crucifix before him like a sword ran from the room. Mina's face reverted to a cruel composition, her eyes tightened and baring her sharpened teeth, she hissed like a scolded cat. The Professor continued his run towards the Count, thrusting the cross into the monster's distorted face. The sudden move sending Dracula back on his heels and tumbling onto the floor. Jonathan moved quickly behind the Professor. They had him. Dracula lay helpless, pressed into the carpet by the crucifix in Van Helsing's hand. Jonathan and the Professor exchanged a glance, both smiling.

40

THE HORRIFIC FIGHT

"You are ours now!" Van Helsing bent over Dracula with the crucifix held firmly towards the face. Mina withdrew her hands before her face. Her jaw clenched and hissing loudly through her teeth. She cowered against the wall furthest away from the melee. "Jonathan, go to my bag and bring it to me. With it we can secure this monster for good." Jonathan, staring at his wife, hesitated for a moment. "Go, now, before it is too late!" He finally turned towards the bedroom holding the Professor's bag.

“It may be too late for you fools; you have pressed me into this!” Dracula growled at Van Helsing.

As he lay with his back pressed against the floor, Dracula motioned with his right hand towards the smaller window in the room that was locked. At that moment, its frame bulged inwards, creaked, and crashed. Glass shattering, spreading splinters and shards onto the carpet beneath it. The wind and drizzle blew into the room like a gale. Loose papers and other items sent into turmoil, spinning and circling before settling quietly around the drama in their new locations.

As the wreckage took its place through the hole that the explosion had created, one figure then another entered the room and hurled themselves to stand behind Van Helsing and Jonathan. Positioning themselves between them and the safety of the bedroom. Jonathan, stopping in his tracks, withdrew closer to Van Helsing as he saw who it was. Jonathan issued a sharp exhalation as he recognized his good friends, Seward, and Godalming, turned now into powerful blood sucking servants of their master.

“John! Arthur! It is me, your friend, help us!”

The vampires stood only for a moment, their flesh pale

and translucent, eyes red with rage and teeth bared over their thin crimson lips. Each focused on their target, ignoring the pleas of recognition. Their obligation and desire were to Dracula. Van Helsing turned and on his face a draw look of horror. He knew that the fight had was lost. Seward lunged at Van Helsing, forcing the crucifix from his hand, sending it tumbling towards the floor. Dracula, seizing his opportunity, struck out with his right arm. Van Helsing off balance fell towards the Count, who caught him gripping the Professor's neck with the claw-like fingers of his left hand raised above his prostrate body. The Van Helsing issued a wheeze as his airway constricted, compressed and broke under the force of the hold.

Dracula, his body as rigid as a board, raised himself off the carpet, leveraging Van Helsing until they were both in an upright position. The Count laughed with a low growl and in an instant plunged his teeth into the jugular. At the same time Godalming had hold of Jonathan, wrapping his arms behind his back and holding them there with a single grip, preventing him from intervening within the melee. Godalming filled himself from Jonathan's neck. Mina left motionless, looking on steadily to Dracula's feeding frenzy, until he released his bite. Mina ran to the limp body of the Professor and licked at the remnants of warm blood as they trickled down the neck. Dracula laughed again, Jonathan now released from Godalming's hold, looked on in disgust and sadness that they had turned his dear wife as he himself knew he had been too.

"Enough my dear, there is more at our place, restrain yourself." At that Dracula lifted the corpse of Van Helsing and threw it headlong out of the open window, before motioning it closed with his hand. The sash obeyed his command, as did all in the room.

Jonathan fell to the floor, collapsing unconscious at what he had witnessed, his spirit broken, his flesh weak. Sensing more blood, the creatures of Seward, followed closely by Godalming, rushed to the bedroom of the boy. They entered, rampaging through its contents, ripping items from the walls, and overturning the bed. Halting as they settled above the place where they knew the boy was hiding, they readied themselves to feast like the animals they were now. Until Dracula called to them.

"Back, back, to the place, you two! Your time is not yet come. We shall all wait! Have patience, my friends! Tonight, that is all mine. Tomorrow night is yours! We need the boy to know what we have done! Hold these two and carry them forward, they are but the bait."

Dracula sweeping his arm to the shattered window opening, signaled to the creatures who were once Seward and Godalming to take Jonathan. They each held an arm, trailing the body behind them, before they leapt out of the gaping hole into the chilly night. The Count brought Mina into his arm, then reaching towards her face, wiped a smudge of Van Helsing's now cold blood from her lips before lifting her boldly so her feet left the ground. Shifting his form into a giant bat, he followed his companions out of the hotel room, sweeping aside the curtains as he twisted through the foggy air and back to the place from which they had come. The hotel room quiet apart from the sound of the now wet drapes slapping the broken frame of the window like a fish drawn from the ocean, caught on the deck of a sinking boat.

41

THE PLAN TRANSLATED

Whatever the plan Sherlock had formed within his mind to being set before our arrival at the hotel was of little consequence. The events now reduced it to nothing more than a thought. Our numbers cut in half and progress set back to the beginning, it seemed. Descending from the hotel room as fast as we were able, we were on the street in front of the hotel in no time, Sherlock holding onto the arm of the boy. We paused for the moment. Sherlock, Lestrade, Quincey and I knew that the time for action had arrived and there was no hiding from what needed to be done.

“Quincey you shall come with us.” Said Sherlock.

“But it cannot be safe for the boy!” Protested Lestrade.

“No safer than anywhere else in this town! He is the next target, the lure on the hook.” Lestrade hesitated, then accepted the course.

“Then where do we go?”

“You return to Scotland Yard, gather your resources and move to clear the upper walkways of the Tower Bridge. You find that the occupants there will be docile and easier to deal with but take care. Although they will appear to be thin and weak, they will have the strength of two men each, and if the darkness may beat you, then they will have even more power than you may imagine, and we all may be lost.”

“What of you three?”

“We shall return presently to 221B and gather our plans from there. I will telegram once we have settled upon the course.”

“It is eleven thirty now. I will have the force in position in three hours to begin the clearance.”

"We need to end this business by four thirty, when the sun sets."

The cab was still waiting outside of the hotel. Sherlock, Quincey and I got in and made haste to return to our quarters. It was just before noon that we arrived back at Baker Street. Sherlock took from his pockets the items that he had collected from Van Helsing's surgical case and laid them upon the breakfast table. He turned to his chair, slumping into it, and took to his pipe. He brought up the small notebook and said, "We need to have a translator to know what this book says, but it is in Dutch!"

"Why, is not Janssen, the store owner below a Dutchman, coming from Rotterdam?"

"Brilliant, my good man. Perfectly brilliant Watson. Now fetch him here with haste!"

I collected Janssen from his store below. He was a well-fed man in his fifties, from a family of merchants who had come to London to escape the trade war between his homeland and England many years before. They had set up business on Baker Street and had become very successful in selling a fine selection of cheeses. Climbing the stairs to the apartment had brought a flush to his cheeks and a sweat to his brow. He removed his flat cloth cap and wiped his forehead with it as he entered the room, revealing his bald shiny scalp, which he also dabbed to dry.

“My good man, please take a seat with us. We need your help.”

“I will see what I can do, but if it is to carry things, or to move furniture then I am not as strong as I used to be.”

“Nothing as exhausting. I have some notes, which I believe are written in Dutch and thus I need help to translate them. You may find the words strange, but it is important that you say what is written, exactly as it reads. Do not shy about it. Do you think you can help?”

“Yes, well, you are correct that I am Dutch, but it is some time that we have used the language. Let me see the words, maybe I can do a little. Where is the book?”

Sherlock passed the notes to Janssen. Holding the book, he flicked through the pages, nodded in affirmation, and read. Quincey sat at the breakfast table and played with his timepiece as he listened in deep thought. I could only have the briefest of empathy towards his situation before my attention returned to the task at hand.

“These notes are a record of the proven protections, antidotes and wapens, could be weapons, I think. The infections of the vampier. The vampier?”

“Yes, carry on. This is good work.”

“A creature that does its business by night, becoming even greater in power with the presence of the full moon. The homes of man are secure from its overtreding as it must at the first make entry only when asked thereto by an inside person. Although in all afterwards he can come when and how he will. Transport over the threshold may be closed by the placing of the herb known as garlic and the sprinkling of Holy wafer.”

“The vampier will seek many hiding places, bringing the soil from his vaderland to lie upon in casket or coffin. The place of his rest will be heavy and well disguised, if finding he will leave to a two, or three places, already there for such a use.”

“If a man is attacked by the animal, the crucifix, being made in the silver, will repel the approach, the power still being felt. Holy water sprayed or dried onto wapens will cause crumbs of the vampire’s flesh if touched. When the vampire is caught at rest, even though in all appearances the body will in appearance be inert the heart must be pierced by a stake. There may writhe and biting so care must be taken to miss contact and be as swift as possible in the action. Once all is subsided, then the head must be cut off from the body and removed. Garlic should be placed in mouth if the form does not scatter, otherwise the dirt and dust should be gesteriliseeerd by the sprinkling of holy wafer."

"My analysis of his present hiding place relates to his original visit. The vampire went from Carfax first to the place where he would suspect delay least. He must have been at Bermondsey or within that area."

Janssen stopped reading with a shudder. "These facts are true? There is such presence of this being? Here in Bermondsey?"

Sherlock relayed to Janssen the facts of the matter and the circumstances that led to the need for us to have the translation. Janssen, without movement throughout the explanation, gradually lost the color from his cheeks, his pallor drained, and beads of perspiration appeared on his forehead. "I shall go now; I must bring some garlic to my rooms from the market."

After Janssen left the apartment, Sherlock returned to the

breakfast table and studied the equipment and tools that we had brought from Van Helsing's bag. He handed each of us a crucifix. "Watson, carry the stakes and the hammer. I shall take the wafers." He turned his attention to the holy water, pouring a small amount into a saucer then handing the remaining to the boy. "Quincey poor some of this water over the blade of your knife." Sherlock took out his revolver and unloaded each of the cartridges. He carefully dipped the tip of each bullet into the saucer, coating them with holy water and setting them aside to dry.

"Now Watson, send a telegram to Lestrade informing him we will be at the south tower of the bridge within the hour and that he should begin with the clearing of the walkways as a matter of some urgency."

Holmes gestured for all of us to gather around the breakfast table. We each faced each other, knowing that it could be the last time that we would do so.

42

THE BRIDGE

"It is a chill evening, and I do not know how long our expedition may last; so, I beg you will wear your warmest and thickest coats. Especially you, Quincey. The weapons that we have are the only protection against the Count and his cohorts. It is of the first importance that we should finish our deed before it grows dark. The moment before darkness arrives is the most dangerous. The vampire will stir from its rest, preparing for its feed and tonight, for its final vengeance upon us all. My brave fellows, with your permission we shall get started at once."

It transformed Sherlock Holmes when he was hot upon such a scent as this. Men who had only known the quiet thinker and logician of Baker Street would have failed to recognize him. His face flushed and darkened. The brows drawn into two hard black lines, while his eyes shone out from beneath them with a steely glitter. His face was bent downward, his shoulders bowed, his lips compressed, and the veins stood out like whipcord in his long, sinewy neck. His nostrils seemed to dilate with a purely animal lust for the chase, and his mind was so absolutely concentrated upon the matter before him that a question or remark fell unheeded upon his ears, or, at the most, only provoked a quick, impatient snarl in reply.

Swiftly and silently, we made our way along the street towards the south tower of the bridge; the gradient inclining to meet the entrance door. A dense London fog would hide the structure from view until we were almost upon it. The boy, Quincey, with a stride half the length of ours, made a little effort in maintaining his position between myself and Sherlock, who was leading.

"Your deductions point to the south tower, Sherlock?"

"Yes, my dear Watson. The tower is in proximity to the wharves from which they take their victims and to St. Olave's workhouse from which they fed and kept as a larder. It is my conjecture that the location of these two resources will fix the position of the lair."

We walked on. The street held a grey fog, a strange arrangement in that a pathway seemed to be carved through its center, an appearance of a tunnel. We approached the Tower Bridge. The upper part of the tower shrouded with the hanging mist like the peak of a mountain top. Further above us, and thus out of our view, the walkways connecting the towers were quiet. The activity of the clearing was abating.

Figures of stragglers found in the Tower emerged like ghosts from the mist. Held securely by a police officer hanging on each arm and pushed into the back of the many wagons that lined the street for this purpose. The darkness was drawing closer and with it, the strength of those captured increased. The wagons rocked back and forth, unsettling the horses before them and causing ripples and swirls in the air. Lestrade and his force had now stopped all traffic from crossing the bridge from both the north and south. The time was near to fifteen minutes before four. Darkness would be upon us in less than one hour.

On entering the main door, we stared down the stairs. A winding spiral descending downwards, further than the light that was available. The stairs themselves hidden from view by the heavy carpet of cascading dense mist. We lit the lamps that we carried; the illumination did not penetrate greater than ten steps before us. The dense, pungent fog prevented the light from finding the stairway further ahead without our decent.

"I will lead." Said Sherlock.

I held onto the polished wood banister rail and wondered whether Dracula's hand had grasped it last before I and stepped into the mist. The fog became thicker and the view more restricted. I was conscious of a hanging, musky odor, subtle and nauseous. At the very first whiff of it, my brain and my imagination were beyond all control. A thick, black cloud of fear swirled before my eyes, my mind told me that in this cloud, unseen as yet, but about to spring out upon my appalled senses, lurked all that was terrifying, all that was monstrous and inconceivably wicked in the universe.

The vampire waited below, dormant on his bed of earth. The fog created vague shapes from the penetration of the light we carried. Abstract forms, real or imagined, swirled, and swam amid the dark cloud bank before our faces. Each shape a menace and a warning of something coming, perhaps the monsters within the Count's control. They would surely come, seeking with outstretched arms the warmth of the bodies and their lifeblood that set to end their existence.

A freezing horror took possession of me. I felt that my hair was rising on the back of my neck, that my eyes were widening to capture any fragment of light, that my mouth was dry with the stench, and my tongue like leather.

The turmoil within my brain was such that something must surely snap. All the incidents that I had witnessed over the last week; the dry, almost mummified body of Seward, the horrific death of Godalming and only this morning Van Helsing crumpled on the cold damp stone. I tried to focus and calm my interior panic and was vaguely aware of some hoarse croak which was my voice, but distant and detached from myself.

At the same moment, in some effort of escape, I broke through that cloud of despair and had a glimpse of Holmes's determined face, fixed upon the destination that lay below. It was that vision which gave me an instant of sanity and of strength. I placed my hand on the shoulder of the boy in front of me; he showed no fear, only six years old, his parents both now lost to Dracula. How could the countenance of such a young soul withstand the horror of this day?

"Quincey, are you steady in our quest?"

"Yes sir. I am. I will do what needs to be done. We cannot solve this without my part. Thus we will solve it. The Count will not rest until I am with them. The irrevocable part of his vengeance. I will not let this monster defeat the name of my family." I couldn't believe that this small boy had the depth of courage to better most grown men.

I lost count of the many steps as the stairs curving and descending into the depths of the tower finally met the small area that led to the place where Dracula slept. Standing at the base of the stairs, the fog swirled about us, making for an eerie moment as we glanced at each other and heard our own hearts beating in the quiet. The destruction of the monster and his slave companions set out in our minds. I examined the determination of the other two, as we all considered the task. Sherlock firm in his posture, with a look of steel upon his brow, the boy Quincey, concentrated and steady, quite a remarkable character contained within such a young frame. We all had our weapons in place and ready to do battle.

Ahead of us, a closed, heavy wooden door, the only separation between us and returning Dracula to the depths of hell. The door had across it at its center and either side above and below that point, three giant steel rods, held in place by substantial iron brackets. We all stepped forward to examine by our touch the barrier that confronted us. The rods themselves, thicker than the length of my thumb, perfectly smooth, containing no grip or hold with which to move them. Each bar embedded firmly into the stone beyond the frame. Dracula had secured the door from entry and it was impossible for us to move.

“The door locked, Sherlock!”

“But from the outside, with no way to move this mechanism.”

“And no keyhole to lead us to a lock. There is no way to pass!”

There was about us a sense of failure, a despair that filled our minds with a darkness that our plan would derail. I pounded my fists into the door in frustration. At that very moment, the bolts holding the door were released, grinding, and then sliding away from their latch with no touch from ourselves.

“You did the job, Watson!”

“I fear the door is in the control of another. The one that begs us to enter.”

Not sure of what the opening would reveal, we all stepped back onto the lowest stair before the door swung slowly inwards. The fog that was previously held like a dam by the entrance flooded into the opening and carpeted the ground. The view above cleared enough to allow, for the first time, the vision of the lair with our own eyes before us. A dark space illuminated by a single flame flickering with a rhythm in the air as it circled around the room. There was no other movement.

“Wait, let me go first.” Sherlock pushed the boy and me to one side as he disappeared before us into the room.

43

THE MECHANICAL ROOM

For a moment all was silence, as Sherlock's footsteps on the stone beneath the translucent mist carpet within the vault halted suddenly.

"Come in, it is clear in here, we need to act before the sun goes below the horizon. We only have a few minutes before he is risen."

The sight that met us was terrifying, but at the same instance, reassuring. It is what we hoped for, a confirmation that we were ahead. In the center of the room an enormous coffin, an ornate throne covered with deep carving depicting vines wrapping over wolves and other beasts of the night. This was no doubt Dracula's bed. Around it, like the spokes of a wheel, six coffins radiated with their heads closest to the center. One of the six smaller than the others, about the length of the boy, Quincey, who stood in silence.

The covers of each were in place. I took the wooden stakes from my shoulder bag. We still had some time to deal with what lay under each lid.

The start would be the one that Dracula would lie in the center sarcophagus. It took an effort to slide the cold stone cover away to reveal the contents. Sherlock was the first to gaze upon the open cask. It was empty, only an imprint in the dirt where the monster would have been.

"It is empty!"

"It cannot be!"

"He has fooled me. He has fooled us all!"

We moved to release the lids of each casket. The two that

were closer to the head of the main box were empty. We then moved to the two outer covers from those. It surprised us to find those occupied.

In the first we found Mina, seemingly just as we had seen her the night before. She was, if possible, more radiantly beautiful than ever; and I could not believe that she was dead. The lips were red, nay redder than before; and on the cheeks was a delicate bloom. Quincey looked on and spoke.

"Is my mother with them?" Sherlock moved his hand into the coffin above Mina's face.

"There may be no hope!" Holmes pulled back the dead lips and showed the white teeth to be even sharper than they were naturally before. "With this and this," and he touched one of the canine teeth and that below it, "the change within the body has progressed to allow the necks of victims to be bitten. I am convinced now that she is with them. Do you observe my poor boy?"

Quincey remained silent. Sherlock took from his pocket the small tin of wafers once held in Van Helsing's possession. "Stand back a moment. To be certain, I will test the state of the spirit as set out by the Professor."

Laying a wafer onto the forehead of the body of Mina, we were stuck by a fearful scream which almost froze our hearts to hear. Placing the Wafer on the waxy skin caused it to sear white hot, a rancid smoke emitting from the contact as it had burned into the flesh as though it had been a piece of molten metal. We all took a step back. Quincy covered his eyes. But only for a moment. There were no tears, only the appearance of a greater determination on his small features.

"Watson, bring a stake and place the point over the heart. You must hammer it through the chest. Then when we begin our prayer for the dead. I shall read it, I have here Van Helsing's book, strike in God's name, that so all may be well with the dead that we love and that the undead pass away."

I took the stake and the hammer, and when once my mind was set on action, my hands never trembled or even quivered. Sherlock opened his missal and read, and Quincey and I followed as well as we could. I placed the point over the heart, and as I looked, I could see its dint in the white flesh. Then I struck with all my might.

The thing in the coffin writhed; and a hideous, blood-curdling screech came from the opened red lips. The body shook and quivered and twisted in wild contortions; the sharp white teeth champed together until the lips cut, and the mouth smeared with a crimson foam. I hit the stake three more times until I felt its passage through the torso and its sudden release into the soft soil below. The blood from the pierced heart welled and spurted up around it. And then the writhing and quivering of the body became less. The teeth seemed to champ, and the face to quiver.

Finally, the thing lay still. The terrible task was over. The remains of the form lay no longer in appearance as the foul thing that we had destroyed, but now as Mina as we had seen her in her life, with her face of unequalled sweetness and purity. True that there, as we had seen them in life, the traces of pain and waste; but these were all dear to us, for they marked her truth to what we knew. One and all we felt that the holy calm that lay like sunshine over the wasted face and form was only an earthly token and symbol of the calm that was to reign forever.

Before the moment was done, Quincey took his knife and carved it with a flash through the neck, releasing the head from its body. He turned to me and said without hesitation or remorse. "We need to release my father as well." And so, we began the same disgusting process. How could the boy have so much inner strength to carry out such deeds? The bodies of the Harker's suddenly aged and disintegrated, the dust falling into the dirt in which they lay.

Sherlock pulled a palm full of wafers from the tin and crumbled them between his fingers into the coffin that had contained Mina. Fragments fell from his hand, twisting and turning in the air before caressing the surface dirt, like a snowfall in the Carpathian Mountains. The dust within frothed and bubbled in reaction, signaling the end to the spirit held in abeyance, gas rising towards the ceiling of the room in a final bow to the world that had now freed her. We all gathered around the inert box and gazed down upon it. The boy showed little emotion other than a slight glassing of his eyes; he stood straight.

"Quincey, this had to be done. Without our action here today these things, you witnessed they were no longer your mother and father would have risen and sought their fill from others. Including you. You know that?" I said. The boy turned his face and looked up directly into mine.

"Yes, sir. They were both gone before now. I know that to be true."

Sherlock motioned to me to place the lid on the coffin and then sliding it into position, we turned our attention to the other box to do the same. We paused for a moment.

"Where do the others lay, Sherlock?" I asked.

Before Holmes could answer, the flame on the wall flickered. Something stirred higher on the stairway.

"Quincy, be quick and enter the smallest box."

In a single jump, Quincey landed within the box. And we pulled its heavy lid to cover, maintaining a faint gap to deliver air to the boy.

"Hold still. We will cover you. Hide within until the business here is finished."

The flame flickered again, a rush of air covered with the dank yellow mist and disgustingly foul smell filled the room.

44

FINAL CONFRONTATION

Sherlock and I turned away from the box. The mist welled to fill the footwell at the threshold of the basement room, pushing into the doorway and holding within it a shape. Emerging through the mist, as though drawing its atoms from the fog, the form became solid, transforming into the outline of a man. Then out of the grey-green-yellow swirling ether stepped Dracula. He was soon flanked on either side by the likenesses of Seward and Godalming.

I shall refer to them as such, because we know nothing remains of the spirit or character of these good men.

Dracula clothed in a dark cloak with its hood revealing only the part of his face below his nose, the thin scarlet lips parting to reveal the sharp white tools that have bled many jugulars.

"Here I am. You followed my will without effort or question. And I congratulate you for doing so. I bring my two good friends so that they can feast on your blood after I have corrupted your spirit" With a contemptuous sneer, they passed quickly through the opening, and we heard the heavy bolts creak as he fastened it behind him with a sweep of his arm. Focusing his eye intently on Sherlock, the same victorious gaze as I witnessed at the Theatre Royal only those four days ago. Four days that passed like minutes in an hourglass, like grains of sand between our fingers.

"So, you, the master of the detective conundrum, choose to play your mind against mine. You would help men to hunt me and frustrate me in my designs! Both of you know now, and so will all of London know, in full before long, what it is to cross my path. You should have kept your energies for use closer to home. Whilst you played your wits against me, against me who commanded nations, and intrigued for them, and fought for them, hundreds of years before they were born. I was countermining them, winning a way past you before any of you could raise a hand to stay me."

Then he came closer. There was something so panther like in the movement, something so unhuman, that it seemed to waken us all from the shock of his coming. The Count flicked the hood from his face, revealing the youngest version of him I could have imagined. The flesh taught, stretched over the sharp features of his face, translucent with the crimson lifeblood bubbling below, eyebrows dark, the eyes piercing, focused as the lion sees the gazelle.

With outstretched arms, his hands pointed to us. The first to act was Godalming, who, with a quick movement, threw himself towards Sherlock. Seward soon followed him, flying towards me. We both reached for our crucifix and held them at shoulder level, halting the vampires with their aim.

They hissed and scratched at the air in front of them. Dracula stood behind them, a horrible sort of snarl passed over his face, showing the teeth long and pointed; but the evil smile as quickly passed into a stony stare of lion like disdain. It was a pity that we had not some better organized plan of attack, for even at the moment I wondered what we were about to do. I did not myself know whether our lethal weapons would avail us of anything.

“When you falter, you will fail.” Shouted Dracula.

“We will wait until the sun rises and then finish what we have started here.” Replied Sherlock.

Instinctively I moved forward with a protective impulse, holding the crucifix. I felt a mighty power fly along my arm; and it was without surprise that I saw the monster in front of me cower back before a similar movement made spontaneously by Sherlock drew the similar withdrawal. It would be impossible to describe the expression of hate and baffled malignity, of anger and hellish rage, which came over the Count’s face.

His waxen hue became greenish yellow by the contrast of his burning eyes, and the red scar on the forehead showed on the pallid skin like a palpitating wound. He threw his hands forward like the conductor of his own orchestra, projecting his power, the force transmitting through the forms of Godalming and Seward pushing against the invisible wall before each crucifix. I felt it compress against my arm. So much that it forced us to step in retreat to the wall and having to use both hands to support our defense. It was a stalemate. How long could we stand? It was a stalemate.

Suddenly, within the quiet of the struggle, a noise echoed through the room. I recognized it immediately. Dracula turned towards the sound, something hidden, a mark of each passing second. A steady ticking of the boy's timepiece. It had revealed its position; the coffin acting as an amplifier of the sound. The Count, smiling, his thin lips drawing over his white sharp teeth, stood over the small coffin reserved for the occupant that it now held.

"There you are. Quite appropriate, Sherlock. What kindness of these men to bring you forward to me, do you not think? Come out of your hiding, Quincey. It is your time to join us all. You are very welcome."

Sherlock and I remained pinned to the wall by the force of attack by Godalming and Seward. I glanced at Holmes. Reducing his grip on the crucifix to one hand, the fingers of his right hand reaching into his coat pocket, they stretched down to grasp its content.

Dracula placed both hands on the lid to the coffin that held the boy and drew it back. The heavy lid flew across the room and smashed against the wall. The boy revealed.

Dracula became in an instant engaged in rapture, laughing with the same deep vibrato that Quincy had heard at the hotel. Quincey, looking up at the ghastly apparition lit by the light of the torch on the wall, withdrew as far as he could into the corner of the case. The back of his head pressing against the soft dirt beneath him. He could not retreat any further. The Count hesitated only a moment before plunging his head towards the neck of Quincey as the boy turned his face away.

There was a stillness in the room. The mist rose in waves from the floor to join in the celebration. I closed my eyes with the knowledge of the disastrous failure that we had brought upon this family. Waiting for the final strike. Then, a gasping exhalation of breath, containing within it a high-pitched animal whimper, echoed in the room. I opened my eyes to look again at the scene, fearful of what I might observe.

Dracula, bending over the casket, jerked upright, his back arching as his head flung itself towards the ceiling. The eyes of the monster bulging, the mouth open, not in conquest, but in terror. Projecting from the monster's chest, the handle and half the length of the blade of the kukri. Quincey sat upright, reached upwards and, gripping the weapon with both hands, pulled it from its target. Dracula folded forward before collapsing at the side of the coffin into the retreating mist. Writhing and aging, decades piling upon his features as he did so. The knife had shorn his heart with a fatal blow. The Count's powerful form reducing to the dust from which it had been resurrected in a matter of seconds.

In that very moment, the creatures embodied as Godalming and Seward became confused; the opportunity allowed Sherlock to take from his pocket his pistol, pushing Godalming away a distance, then raising his aim. Holmes let off a shot, which entered the vampire's forehead with a sickening crack as the impact shattered the brittle bone of the skull.

The bullet dipped in the holy water taken from Van Helsing's bag did more damage than anyone could have expected. The hole from where it entered the head rapidly increased in size, the flesh and bone around it crumbling away as though being eaten by some parasite. I could see right through the center of the head where the face had been. The process quickly engaging the whole body as it too crumbled into particles into the mist that swirled around the floor.

Quincey leaping from his hiding place took the kukri and ran it down the spine of Seward as he was still in mid-air, his weight carrying him downwards until his feet found the floor. The ribs separating from the backbone splayed as the wings of an angel, twisting Seward to face his attacker. The knife swiftly withdrawn and with an arc flashed through the neck and the windpipe.

I moved forward and thrust a stake through the torso of Seward, aiming at the position of the heart. It struck home, releasing a deep moan from the gaping throat. The body arching and disintegrating as the others. The mist withdrew in reverse from the lair and shrank upwards along the staircase. Outside we could hear the howling of dogs, before a sudden silence to the whole of the city.

All those involved in the destruction of Dracula for the first time in the Carpathian Mountains were now dead. The boy, Quincy, confirmed an orphan, stood with the kukri dripping with the rancid scarlet lifeblood of his victims in one hand and the loudly ticking timepiece in the other. He looked at me and then to the ashes of the now dissipated bodies that laid around our feet and within the coffins, then said with a look of promise and determination.

"There is more to do Watson, this city has a contamination. And I, Quincy, Jonathan, Arthur, John, Abraham, Harker shall be the one to clean it."

EPILOGUE

It is seven years since we dispatched Dracula and his evil cohorts. Turning them to the dust from whence they came. I will always hold close to my heart the help and friendship that I received from Mr. Holmes and Dr. Watson during that dreadful week and thereafter. Caring for me and then placing me with a loving family until my mission with destiny could begin. I have, by my side those horrific memories of the week that took my parents and their friends.

The century turned with a new beginning, a hopeful light amongst the darkness. Tower Bridge has returned to keeping within its use. But tonight, I carry with me the kukri of my father, its blade bathed in holy water. I hold it close, together with the timepiece that has marked faithfully the passage of each second until this moment. I always understood that its hands would eventually point to the moment of battle as it arrives.

The accounts of Dr. Watson and the journals will help my search to rid the Earth of all the foul creatures who remain to rule the hours of darkness. I have educated myself in the way of the vampire. Using the notes of Professor Van Helsing as my guide I have come to this point. My journey has brought me to this place of sacred burial. The foggy grounds of Frogmore Park. I will not rest until all such creatures are destroyed.

Quincey Harker, February 4th, 1901

www.ingramcontent.com/pod-product-compliance
Lightning Source LLC
Chambersburg PA
CBHW010451310726
48979CB00013B/2157/J

* 9 7 8 1 7 3 6 5 7 0 9 5 1 *